The Da
Microp
A Novel By
Sa'id Salaam

DARK PRINCE 2

First edition. April 12, 2020.

Written by Sa'id Salaam.

"Kristine Musa, Interpol forensic special operations," a lovely lady said when she entered the Fulton County coroners office. She held up her credentials but no one was looking. Instead, the male doctors looked at her pretty, light brown face, her plump breast under the white blouse straining to be free. The curve of her hips in the pants suit begged for attention, as well. Her thick, naturally curly hair was courtesy of her mixed East Indian and African heritage.

"You're the vampire lady!" a young tech gushed when he came in and recognized the woman.

"I've never been called that before," Kristine chuckled lightly. She understood the power her beauty had on men. She even seduced a vampire once. She gained his trust and shared his bed until she was able to drive a wooden stake through his heart. She was as dangerous as she was gorgeous. She had to be since she hunted monsters for a living.

"Yes, you have. Interpol said they were sending the vampire lady," the medical examiner said when he shook off the initial shock of her beauty. The type of beauty that pressed the pause button when she walked into a room.

"Well, can I see the victim?" she insisted since that's why she was here. She'd flown nonstop from Egypt when she heard of another bloodless body.

"Sure, but I have to warn you, it's gruesome," the doctor warned. The sight of Shay even threw him for a loop. That's saying a lot in a violent city like Atlanta where the AK 47 was the weapon of choice.

The lady doctor tilted her head and smirked at his remark. It was a tacit way of saying, "Mister, you have no idea what gruesome really is". She may have looked like she was in her early twenties but was in her mid thirties and had been doing this for over a decade. A decade of travelling the world and investigating the gruesome remains left behind by vampires.

1

Gruesome is what she did to vampires when she caught them. The brilliant woman was working on a cure for the virus of vampires but it had a ways to go. Until then, she cut off heads, burned alive, shot with silver bullets, drove wooden stakes through hearts or trapped outside in the deadly sun.

"Alrighty then," he said and pulled the sheet away from Shay's empty shell. The tech rushed away to upchuck it into a trashcan when he saw the angle of her twisted legs that had been forced out of their sockets.

"Ah..." Kristine said and zeroed in on the two distinct holes in her inner thigh. It lined up perfectly with her femoral artery. She nodded her curly head at the telltale sign of a vampire. "Was there any blood left in her?"

"Not a drop. Her organs had even collapsed, but..." he said because he didn't believe in vampires. He didn't have an answer to this strange finding but whatever it was, wasn't a vampire.

"Hmph?" she asked herself although she was convinced. There was a vampire in Atlanta. She wasn't sure if it lived here or was just passing through. She recalled reading reports about a trucker/vampire who spread his carnage across the country and back. He was found headless in a Charlotte truck stop thirty or forty years ago.

Whoever he or she was, Kristine Musa was on his or her ass now.

CHAPTER 1

Angela opened one eye to peek at the clock when her man came in. She never checked him about the time but did keep track. She didn't think he would cheat but still sniffed for sex when he got in bed. He didn't get right in bed though.

"Uh uhh!" Meech grunted as he made it rain hundreds on Angela in the bed.

"Meechie! What did you do?" she whined and looked towards the door, assuming the police would be barging in behind him. She couldn't remember the last time he had two hundred dollars bills at the same time, let alone a whole heap of them.

"I did what I said I would do! I got me an artist! He dope, too! Rap, sing, pretty boy, the whole package! Baby we finna be rich!" he declared.

"Good, cuz I'm tired of slinging chicken," she sighed. She had heard this before but it never came with cash. "So, how you get paid already?"

"Dirt. He tried to chump me off and give me ten grand for my artist! I told him hell naw! Then Matt was like you need to give him to us, but Prince was, like "Nah, I'm rolling with Meech, and..."

Angela tuned most of it out since it didn't matter. She smiled softly and imagined a better life for her family. She could finally quit her job and get away from her nasty boss. The man forced her to give him a hand job for some overtime. She got some extra hours but felt like a cheater.

"That's wonderful, baby," she interrupted and placed his hand between her thick legs.

"And then I..." he was saying, but abandoned it at the prospect of some pussy. Meech wasn't very creative in the sack but sometimes that's okay. He and Angela always made love face to face. No fancy positions, flips or tricks, but it got the job done. The couple copulated copiously and concluded with a combined climax. They cuddled up and drifted off to sleep until morning or their daughter woke up. Whichever came first.

*****

Meanwhile, Prince was on the prowl for something to eat. He bypassed a late night taco joint and several waffle spots. A round ass switching through a 24-hour gas station caught his eye, so he pulled in for a closer look.

The woman heard a car pulling in and put a little extra on her walk. A little goes a long way with a fat ass and Prince pulled up. He needed gas, so he would kill three birds with one stone. Fill his tank, get his rocks off and feed.

"Need some company?" the young chick playing woman of the night asked with a hand on her hip. Prince loved young victims since they were tender like veal, or spring lambs.

"I sure—" Prince was saying as two goons popped out of their ambush spot. They were waiting until he inserted the nozzle in his tank and rushed him.

"You know what it is, nigga!" one shouted, while pointing his gun at Prince's face.

"Come off that money, watch, and I want yo' car!" the other teen shouted while pointing his gun at his head.

The girl raised her hands but Prince still checked what was on her mind to see if she was down with the lick. Bait for the trap, since the goons were around her age. She wasn't, but he still frowned by what he saw. They could talk about that later since these boys wanted his attention.

"As I was saying," Prince said and turned back to the wannabe prostitute. A lot of young urban girls slung a little pussy on the side for a variety of reasons. Some were just too lazy to work but wanted bundles and clothes. Others were running from abuse in the home. "I would love some company. Hop in."

"Nigga, you think this a game?" the first kid shouted at being ignored, and caused Prince to laugh in his face.

"Yes, and a very dangerous one at that. Now go on home and get some sleep," Prince advised. He didn't have to read their minds since the malice was written all over their faces. They made their choice to shoot, so Prince shrugged and made a slight mental adjustment.

The teens turned their weapons towards each other's faces just before they fired. Their heads snapped back from the impact of the slugs and dropped dead on the spot. The young woman shouted at the carnage but Prince just filled his tank.

"Get in," he said and topped his tank off and went inside the station.

"What the fuck!" the clerk said from behind the bulletproof partition.

"I know, right?" Prince laughed then peered into his irises until he reached his soul. "Give me the video."

The man turned and quickly complied to the order as Prince watched on. He retrieved the disk from the computer and handed it over. Prince gave a nod and walked out and got behind the wheel.

"Did they really shoot each other?" the girl asked as he pulled away from the scene.

"Yeah," Prince giggled. He took the tape mainly to keep police from seeing it. It would clear him of any wrongdoing but would bring unwanted attention. Besides that, he wanted to keep it for his own amusement.

"Wow!" she said and rode in silence all the way over to Prince's Westside home. She 'wowed' again when she entered his well appointed house. Then again when they reached his room and he pulled out his dick.

"Um?" he said and wagged his wood at her.

"Oh yeah!" she laughed when she remembered what she was here for. She had a shock for him as well when she stepped out of her clothing.

"Whoa!" he said when she revealed her picture perfect body. Her big firm breast stood up proudly when she removed her bra. A thick tuft of curly pubic hair covered a plump mound of good young pussy. She giggled at his reaction then reached for the dick dangling in front of her.

"Whoa!" Prince repeated when he watched his dick disappear down her throat. A third "whoa" was drowned out by her gags. He wondered if she wasn't trying to commit suicide by choking herself to death on his dick. She worked her head, lips, tongue, and hand in perfect harmony. It got better when she spit his dick out and worked his balls while stroking the shaft. She pulled every dick trick out of her sleeves until he skeeted down her throat.

"Yay!" she cheered at her own handiwork. Prince pushed her back on the bed to see what was under that afro between her legs.

"Whoa!" he said once more as he inched his inches inside of her. She gripped the sheets and grimaced, and took the dick. He gave her all he had and she took it like a champ.

"Shit!" the girl shouted as the first orgasm of her life wracked her body and rocked her world. Prince felt her contractions and bust inside of her. He never worried about birth control since he always drank his bedmates.

"What is your name and why are you on the streets?" he asked since she didn't fit the bill of the average street walker.

"Roshawn and I need the money," she said out loud but he went into her head and got the rest. A slight snarl twisted the corner of his mouth as he watched her memory of her stepbrother and stepfather sneaking into her room at night and having their way with her. He planned to pay them both a visit and soon.

"I'm not even hungry anymore," Prince laughed to himself. Little did she know that good pussy just saved her life.

"I am," she pouted. She just ate plenty of dick but that can't fill a belly.

"Get dressed," he ordered and stepped into his bathroom to rinse the sex away. They stepped outside and looked towards the sky. Dawn was close so he only took her as far as the Marta station. He handed her her pay when he pulled to a stop.

"All this!" she shrieked at the stack of cash he gave her. It was more than she had ever held in her life.

"All that, and my number. Call me when you need more. Stay off the streets," he warned.

"Yes sir," she complied without the hypnosis. She leaned over and kissed his cheek before running off to catch the approaching train.

Prince turned to go home and feed off a packet of plasma from his fridge but a skinny junkie ran up and knocked on the window. He wasn't too fond of junkies since he could taste the impurities and diseases in their blood. He was immune but wasn't fond of the taste. They were the late night version of crystals and worked in the clutch.

"Hop in," he said and popped the lock so she could. He pulled around the corner while she bantered.

"I got the best head on the block. I..." she was saying until the vampire attacked. His fangs cut through the chatter and into her jugular veins. The plasma would wait for another day as he drank his fill.

Prince almost pushed the empty body out the door like an empty soda cup. He caught himself and took her home to dispose of her properly. Good thing, too, because a vampire hunter was in town looking for empty bodies.

CHAPTER 2

"What you doing?" Meech asked when he saw Angela putting her uniforms in the garbage.

"Putting my uniforms in the garbage," she said. Sometimes a woman has to fall back and let a man be a man and that time had come. Angela took him at his word and quit his job. She held the family down long enough and now it was on him.

"Good!" he nodded. He was able to get his car fixed with his sudden windfall. Half went to her since she paid the bills. The woman wasn't a fan of fancy stuff and showing off, so she would make it last.

"So, what now?" Angela asked since this was as far as Meech had ever gotten in the music world.

"Now we gotta work out a deal with Dirt. Then get into the studio and make some hits," he said since he knew that much. This would be his first deal, so he mulled over what to ask for and what to give up.

"Hmph!" she huffed at the mention of his cousin's name. She hated the way he looked down on her man whenever they were together. Even when he threw Meech a few bucks it was like he was a beggar.

"I know," he said since he knew how she felt about him. He also knew the hits were the easy part. It was dealing with his cousin that would be the problem.

"Well, handle that, daddy," she giggled and went to tend to their child. Once night fell, Meech set out to meet his client so they could strike a deal.

"Finna get me a Bentley, too!" he vowed to himself since his cousin had one. He shook his head and decided to one up him and get a Rolls Royce. Why not since Prince was ten times the artist that Dirt was? Dirt Jones was a gimmick and gimmicks don't last.

The Dark Prince was the real deal. He had the look, the sound, and the songs. Meech was still singing his praises when he arrived at the restaurant they were supposed to meet up at. He parked a block away since his old car didn't quite fit in with the fancy ones outside the eatery. He spotted Prince sitting alone on the outside patio as he approached.

"Hey, Prince!" he cheered and waved as he crossed the street. Meech was smiling so hard, his chubby cheeks closed his eyes, so he didn't see the SUV speeding towards him.

Prince did and saw it actually sped up as it neared. It would have been a fatal hit and run had the driver not made the fatal mistake of glancing over at Prince. He suddenly snatched the wheel and slammed into a light pole. The driver wasn't wearing a seatbelt since he was only here to run a pedestrian down. He slammed into the dash and windshield causing some fatal wounds of his own.

"Oh shit! Oh shit!" Meech repeated at the near death experience and got his ass out the street. It came so close that he felt himself up to make sure he was still intact.

"Oh shit!" Dirt cussed as he watched from his Bentley parked up the block. He let out a sigh and pulled up for their meeting.

"This dude had one job," Matt moaned from the passenger seat.

"They don't teach to look left, right and left again anymore?" Prince asked when Meech joined him on the patio. Technically, he was supposed to go through the restaurant but the accident took enough attention for him to hop the partition.

"Nah, that's like the old days. That was close! I almost died!" he said. Prince peeked inside his head and realized he didn't put that two together with the two walking up to them now. In fact, all he had was positive thoughts floating around. Prince almost smiled at Meech's thoughts of buying his daughter some toys. Almost that is because Dirt and Matt just arrived.

"Sup, Prince, Meech," Dirt said stoically. He wasn't even a good enough actor to hide his disappointment at not killing his cousin.

"Dirt," Prince greeted, took his hand and took a sneak peek inside his mind. All he saw was malice and misery bouncing around in his cranium. He practically snarled at his cousin, seeing he was still breathing.

"Yo, that was crazy!" Matt said to break up the awkward silence. He raised his hand to summon a waitress and they all sat. The awkward silence threatened to start again since Dirt's whole spiel revolved around Meech being splattered in the street.

"Ready to talk some business?" Prince asked as he pulled out the paperwork. He took the liberty of drawing up contracts between himself and his manager as well as the joint label deal with Dirt.

"Yeah, I was gonna do... un huh, yeah," Meech said as they all reviewed the iron clad management contract.

"Transferable to his girl? Ten million dollar buy out! Twenty year deal?" Dirt moaned as he read the contract that protected Meech, dead or alive. If Meech died, he still wouldn't get his piece of the Prince pie. Actually, it was about to be a whole cake. Lots and lots of cake.

"Yeah," Prince smiled and attracted several women and a couple of men around the patio. He had the attention of many but only one had his.

A woman sitting with her husband a few tables away flirted so hard, the man turned to see what she was smiling at. He let out an exasperated sigh like, *Here we go, again*. Prince tuned out whatever Dirt was saying since it didn't matter. Meech signed his copy of the signed copy and it was written in stone. He instead tuned into the thoughts coming from the couple a couple tables away.

Hey, handsome. I wish my boring husband would just drop dead right here on the spot. We can use his body as a mattress and fuck right on top of him, she thought and smiled softly at the morbid thought.

Bruh, you can have her. She's pretty and the sex is bananas, but she ain't worth a damn. I lost all my friends behind her since she fucked them all. Wish it was her in that truck, he thought back and smiled. They casually wished each other the worst as they ate the best tacos in the city.

"Oh and here's our deal. It's one of those take it or leave it type of deals," Prince explained as he passed copies all around. Except to Matt, since he only said yes when Dirt told him to say yes.

Why didn't I think of that? Meech shouted inside his head as he read the point structure.

How I'm supposed to screw you like they screwed me? Dirt wondered as he read those same conditions. It was something rare in the music biz a fair contract.

"I'on like the—" Dirt began and Prince began to stand. "Where you going?"

"Home. Since you 'ont like something. Whatever," Prince shrugged like it was no big deal. It wasn't since he had the power of hypnosis and could make him do whatever he wanted. Still it was more fun to force his hand the old fashion way and make him do it on his own.

"Nah, I don't like this font! I'm a New Times Roman dude myself. I like it. I like it!" he shouted and turned a few heads. He would still make a million or two instead of the tens of million he stood to make from the deal he had in mind. The same deal he signed when he started that had his manager eating better than he was.

"Well, let's sign on the dotted line. I may have a date tonight," Prince said as the married woman gave a French Fry some head to show him what she was working with. Her husband saw it too and stood. He was too dignified to cause a scene but too proud to sit there and take it.

Dirt shook his head in disbelief as he signed his name and the deal was done. Meech was all teeth and gums when it settled in that he had made it. It didn't escape him that Prince negotiated his own deal but he was still the proud recipient of twenty percent of his income. Now they had to get down to work.

"We can do something with my girls next. Them girls can sing!" he declared.

"Bury they faces in the sand. Them bitches are hit!" Dirt laughed. Matt laughed too but Prince paid attention to Meech. He had a good heart and wanted to help the girls. Prince did too now. How ugly could they really be?

"A'ight, cuz. Hit me up when you ready to get us in the studio," Dirt said and stood.

"ASAP!" he shot back and stood. The men exchanged pounds and went their separate ways. Prince stayed behind to meet his dinner.

"Well, hello there!" the woman smiled and greeted as he took the seat her now estranged husband had just vacated. "I'm Amanda."

"Prince," Prince said and peered into her eyes. He saw nothing good in her and knew he had a meal. He would fuck her for desert and then eat her for dinner.

"I would have thought you were a king," she complimented and batted her eyes. All unnecessary since she had already been selected.

"Let's get out of here," he suggested and stood. She tossed back the rest of her drink and stood, as well. Prince smiled since alcohol makes the blood thin and flow easier. She wobbled slightly and followed him out to his car.

Prince decided to do her husband a favor and took her to a hotel instead of his home. Using his crematorium would ensure she was never found and he wanted her to be found.

"Was that your husband?" he asked even though he knew the answer. It was just small talk to fill the space between the restaurant and the hotel.

"Yes, with his soft ass. Ugh! He can't handle a woman like me. I sleep around and he does nothing! Had another man's baby on him and he does nothing!" she ranted. Prince lost one of his appetites as he listened to her rant about her husband. She hated the man for being a good man. Prince was awfully self righteous for a monster.

"Here we are," he cut in when they reached their destination. They rented a room and went inside. Amanda immediately began to strip the moment he closed the door behind them. He went into the bathroom and ran a hot bath while she undressed. She was still running her mouth about her husband when she slid into the tub.

Prince almost changed his mind when he got a look of her in her birthday suit. He could punish her with the dick, but she would still get some pleasure and she didn't deserve it.

"Aren't you going to join me?" she pouted when he hadn't began to undress.

"Nah," he said and pulled her wrist up to his mouth to drink from the tap.

"Kinky!" Amanda giggled. She enjoyed sordid sex she found around town while her husband stayed home but this was new, and painful. She really didn't like it when he used his claw to slit both her wrist. "I don't think I like this?"

He drank from one while the other turned the water red. Prince ignored her protest and continued to drink. He almost got carried away but caught himself when she passed out from lack of blood. It looked like she took her own life in the tub.

"You did the world a favor," he told the soon to be corpse and left the room. A pack of plasma would top him off once he got home but he still had another thirst to quench.

*****

"Thanks for coming to get me," Roshawn said stoically when she hopped in the passenger seat.

"My pleasure," he said since she was already leaning over to remove him from his pants and get him into her mouth.

Her stepfather and brothers had trained the girl by literally running trains on the girl. They fucked her for free and she still went hungry and without. She turned to the streets to do the same thing she did at home but got paid for it.

"I think I'll keep you," Prince decided as her head bobbed below. She managed a smile despite a mouthful of dick, then through it into overdrive. He rewarded her with a protein shake and resumed the ride to his house.

Once they arrived, Prince took her upstairs and rocked her to sleep. He dressed in all black and headed back into the night. He could move must faster on foot than his car which would draw attention if he sped across town. Instead, he transformed into a black blur and headed to Roshawn's house.

"Hope that's her!" Benny said when he heard the front door open and close.

"I got first!" his older brother, Walt, insisted. Benny could only suck his teeth since he was regulated to sloppy seconds.

"I got first!" their father, David, announced when he came out. Benny sucked his teeth again as he slipped to thirsty thirds.

"You do have first," Prince agreed as he stepped into the room. The men all opened their mouths to protest, but Prince shut them up with his mind. "Now, since you like head so much..."

Benny frowned when he was lost control of his body. He was unable to prevent himself from going over and going down on his father. Prince commanded Walt to join in so he did.

"I'll have a look around," Prince said since the three were busy with their threesome. The family lived in poverty, so Roshawn was their main source of entertainment. He was still shocked to see her mother in her bed watching TV.

"Who are you?" the nearly five hundred pound woman asked in labored breaths. The fat in her throat actually gurgled when she spoke. Prince's fangs slid out automatically. The vampire's version of an instant erection.

All vampires know virgins have the best blood but were hard to find in adults. Babies fit that bill but only monsters drank the sweet blood of infants. Third on the list would have to be the obese. Most were diabetic, which gave them a sweet taste, as well. Some fat people tasted like red liquorice and who doesn't love liquorice. Other tasted like cake or even sweet potato pie, and everyone loves sweet potato pie.

"Oh my!" he said and blinked like it was too good to be true. He was happy he didn't drink too much so he could have some room.

"Are you gone rape, me?" she asked hopefully as he approached. She hadn't had any dick from her husband since her daughter reached puberty. He was looking right up her tent-sized nightshirt at her big thighs.

"Absolutely not," he said and pushed her large legs apart. He licked his lips and leaned in to feed.

"Ouch!" the woman said when he bit through the fat and found her femoral artery. A satisfying flow of sweet blood began to fill his mouth. It was like a Thanksgiving meal as he gorged himself. She didn't protest and let him feed.

"I'll see you again, soon," he said as he stood. He couldn't drain the large woman if he had tried. Instead, she would be a sweet treat for special occasions.

"Okay," the woman said and drifted off to sleep. Walt and his brother were still blowing their father when Prince returned.

"Kill yourselves," he suggested as he passed through the room. David retrieved his trusty revolver and pressed it against his temple. A tug on the trigger sent a .38 caliber slug speeding through his head.

He and the gun fell but Benny picked it up and did the same thing. Walt frowned since he didn't want to but was unable to stop himself. He pried the gun from his brother's hand and fired a round into his head, as well. Prince would keep Roshawn long enough to miss the crime scene. Then he could quench his hunger and thirst in the same place. He could fuck the daughter and drink from the mother.

CHAPTER 3

"You be vamping, huh?" Meech asked when Prince pulled up to the studio.

"What do you mean?" he asked intently. He leaned in to listen to his mind just in case he said something other than what was on it.

"Like you like to record all night. Like a vampire," he explained. He had to just explain it to his woman who wanted him in bed beside her at night.

"Oh," Prince smiled in relief. He liked the man but would feed on him and feed him into his crematorium rather than let his secret get out. He learned from Katrina that his survival depended upon his secrecy. "Yeah, vamping."

"Well, let's get to it then!" Meech said and led the way inside the studio building.

The record label that owned Dirt and now Prince also owned half the acts in town. As a result, they bought a huge building on the industrial side of the city to house their studio complex. Hobos and crack hoes milled around the gated complex like a scene from the Walking Dead.

"Room B," a guard advised when they stepped inside.

"B? OK, B. B is good," Meech nodded and looked around for a clue which way room B was.

"Right next to room A," the guard said and pointed down the hall.

"That's right, B! I had thought you said..." Meech laughed and led the way. Prince let him lead even though he knew he'd never been there before. He had never made it this far in the industry but he was there now.

"Look," Prince said and paused just before they entered. "Stay loyal. Don't cross me and I'll make you rich."

Prince went inside his head once again and saw nothing but honesty and loyalty as his large head nodded up and down. They shook on it and went inside. The large room was dominated by a huge, mixing console. It was flanked by all kinds of modules with blinking lights and knobs. Keyboards were stacked three high on three stands. Meech felt slightly light headed when they walked in. Meanwhile, Prince's dick got hard since he loved this shit.

"Here they are!" a light skinned man with long dread locs announced with a hint of sarcasm. Meech picked up on it and showed some of that loyalty in his client's defense.

"Session don't start until the Dark Prince is in the building!" he said loud and proud and looked to Prince for approval.

"Word. Anyway, I'm Prince," he said and extended his hand.

"Adam Salah. I'm your producer and engineer," he replied. Now it was Meech's turn to fan girl when he recognized one of the hottest producers in the game.

"Cuz pulled out the big guns, huh!" Meech cheered. The hit maker in front of them guaranteed them a hit. His name on a track guaranteed radio play in every market in every city.

"Nah, the label did. They got ahold of the video from the showcase," he explained. "So you better bring your A game!"

Little did the two mortal men know, Prince had been doing this for decades. He had sat in on studio sessions from the eighties with RunDMC and Public enemy, the nineties with NWA and Ice Cube, then again down in New Orleans when Cash Money became millionaires.

As a result, he was quick and proficient in the booth. Once they picked a few tracks, he stepped into the soundproof booth. Adam would pull them up and Prince would knock them down. An hour before dawn and they had three hit records in the bag.

"How about, this..." Adam asked and pulled up another track. All heads bobbed but it was not to be. At least not tonight.

"Next time, burn me a copy and I'll write something to it," Prince said since a beep on his watch alerted him to the approaching dawn.

"But we rolling!" the producer protested. He was one of those lab rats who practically lived behind a mixing board. Plus, he got paid by the beat now, then again with half the publishing when it hit the airwaves. Last, Prince was everything they said he was and he wanted him all to himself.

"Yeah, well..." Prince said over his shoulder as he walked towards the door. He had gotten enough out of the producer's head to know that he was the man. They would work around his nocturnal lifestyle.

"I guess I can put a mix on some of these?" Adam asked and answered himself with a nod. A real engineer will turn knobs and twist dials for days after a song has been laid.

"I guess I'll go on home too then," Meech announced since he had no reason to stay. He only hoped it was one of those golden hours when his girl was up and his baby was sleep, so he could get him some late night loving.

*****

Prince awoke late afternoon and stretched. He no longer urinated but still woke up with a piss hard on. It was afternoon wood since he didn't do mornings anymore. Morning was the new night and he was just turning in.

"Let's see what you guys have been up to?" he said and turned to the news. He could always count on the city's high crime rate to amuse him. It also helped hide his own thirst for blood.

"Another bloody night in Atlanta..." the pretty reporter reported with an incongruent smile. She relayed the latest deaths to add to the record setting year as if giving the weather report.

"I need to check them out," Prince mused in response to a gang war on the city's south side. The bloodletting would be a smorgasbord for the vampire.

He spent the rest of the day writing songs and watching gory movies. Meech disturbed his groove shortly before nightfall.

"You ready to lay some more heat!" he cheered when Prince answered. He was so excited, he didn't register his response until halfway through his next sentence. "They all singles too but we.... wait, what?"

"Not tonight. I have some research to do," he repeated since he missed it the first time.

"I—I, umm, okay," Meech said, stuttering. He wouldn't mind staying home with his family. At the rate they laid down songs last night, the project would be done in no time flat. "I'll just see you tomorrow then, playboy!"

"Tomorrow night," Prince agreed and clicked off. He dressed to kill and set out to do just that.

Prince drove over to where he kept his play car parked since he didn't want his main car to be seen near too many crime scenes. Not to mention the shiny, new car drew too much attention. It was a magnet for young chicks, but he wasn't hunting for pussy tonight.

He switched cars and drove down to the south side of town. The sounds of gunfire in the thick summer night air directed him to the hood like a tour guide. A police cruiser cruised right by like it didn't hear the shots ringing, and he knew he was in the right spot.

Two local gangs shared one large apartment complex on Campbellton road. They were very similar to him in that they slept by day and killed by night except they lived with grandmamas and baby mamas. Oh and Prince killed to eat while they killed for sport. Most times because tonight Prince planned to do both.

He saw the two factions had literally drew a line in the sand using spray paint on the asphalt. He parked since he needed to be up close and personal. It was good timing as the groups both took cover behind their neighbors and aunties cars and began shooting at each other. Prince became a blur as he moved in to help the matters along.

"Hey!" a thug whined when Prince lifted him up from his crouched position. He was straight in the line of fire and someone fired at him.

"Nice shot!" Prince remarked when the boy was hit in his throat. The bullet knocked his Adam's Apple away and allowed Prince to drink straight from the ragged wound.

He made sure not to drink too much since the night was young and bodies were dropping on both sides. Prince felt his pulse slow to the point of no return and dropped him. He rushed across enemy lines and caught another body before it reached the ground.

"Help me," the wounded man pleaded. The gaping wound in his chest was courtesy of an AK 47.

"Sure," Prince said and stuck his mouth into the flow of blood. He tossed that one to the side and fed on another before he died. The gunfire stopped as quickly as it started and tonight's battle was over.

One man limped away with a nonfatal leg wound. It became fatal when Prince spotted him and sped to his side.

"Arrrgh!" the man screamed as the monster dragged him on the side of the building. Prince was more animal than man during the furious feeding frenzy. He bit away most of the man's calf muscle and held him upside down with one hand while he fed.

"What the fuck!" a man shouted when he came across the gory sight. Prince snarled and let out a roar that could be heard from a mile away. The feeding subsided and he slowly transformed back into a man.

"Well, that was fun," Prince said as he got back into his car and drove away from the scene. His next stop would be Roshawn's cervix since he couldn't get any deeper inside her than that.

*****

"Sup, bruh. You up?" Meech asked when Prince took his call. He made sure to wait until after noon before making the call.

"Yeah," Prince drawled lazily as Roshawn gave him some head for the road. They had sex until the dawn and drifted off to sleep. She offered a going away blowjob present before her Uber arrived.

"Good. I got us a few shows lined up! May as well build a buzz and make some dough while we recording the album," he suggested. Come to find out ten thousand dollars isn't as much as it seems to people who never had ten thousand dollars. The family was so far behind and so much in need, they ran through it rather quickly.

"Local only," Prince agreed. He'd been on some of the biggest tours in rap history over the last thirty years. He looked forward to going again since it allowed him to spread his carnage far and wide.

"Okay, local only! We in the studio tonight?" he asked and crossed his fingers.

"We are in the studio tonight!" Prince said and could see him pumping his fist through the line. He hung up and fed Roshawn her brunch.

"When can I see you again?" she with a pout and a belly full of babies.

"Soon," he answered like he always did as the car service sent alert from outside. It was enough to put a smile on her face as she left the house and went home. A home a lot more peaceful since the bizarre murder suicide that claimed her stepdad and brothers.

CHAPTER 4

"Prince laid down four more songs. He halfway down with his project," Matt said, hoping to inspire his boss. Dirt only managed to get high and get two more girls pregnant during that same time. He made the mistake of listening to what Prince laid down and knew he couldn't compete.

"Man, fuck Prince. Fuck Meech, fuck the Braves, the Falcons..." he said and paused to drink Hennessey straight from the neck of the bottle. "Fuck this music shit!"

"Now you just talking crazy! We finna finish this album. Go on tour and fuck some bitches! That's what we finna do!" Matt said and finally took charge. He had some more but a knock on the door pressed pause on his spiel. He was still a flunkie, so he rushed to open the door. "P, p, prince?"

"Just Prince. You can keep the extra Ps. Sup, Dirt?" he said and sauntered in.

"Sup," Dirt said semi cordially. He had no idea the vampire heard all the foul words bouncing around in his head. The smile on his face did nothing to mask the malice in his mind.

"So, look. I know I'm a rookie and all, but I was wondering, hoping if I could um, get you on a song with me?" Prince asked, displaying he was quite the actor, too. Dirt was still in heavy rotation so being on a song with him would be the perfect introduction to the world.

"Hell, yeah!" Dirt cheered and showed his hand. Little did he know his services on the planet would no longer be needed once he put Prince on.

"Cool. Swing by room B tomorrow night and we'll make it happen,"

"And it's finna be fiyah!" Dirt cheered like a groupie. Matt was embarrassed for him but it did give him the motivation he needed to get in the booth to record his next album. Not knowing it would be his last album.

Prince laid down a few new songs and was closer to completion. Meech was looking for girls with the right sound and right looks to sing back up on quite a few songs. The only girls he knew were butt ugly.

"Well, I'm out," Prince announced after he returned to room B and filled them in on Dirt agreeing to record a song with him. The night was still young and Prince was hungry.

"Okay. I'ma stay here for a while," Meech said casually. He had no idea Prince could read his mind. He smiled softly at his not so secret surprise and left.

*****

"Nah. Un uh. Oh, hell no!" Prince said as he cruised the downtown Atlanta streets in search of a meal. He turned his nose up a skinny crack head that tried to wave him down. They were good for a snack but sometimes it took two or three for him to get full. Then declined a middle-aged woman who looked like she would be missed if she went missing. Missing white women made national headlines and he didn't want those problems.

The "oh, hell no" was when he flat out refused the six foot sissy who winked from the line of a gay bar. Atlanta was a gay city, so he didn't discriminate. He could smell the HIV coursing through the man's system from the street. Prince was immune from it as well as all other diseases but the virus had a bitter aftertaste like saccharin.

"Is that her?" he asked when he saw a four hundred pound woman enter the donut shop. He whipped to a stop and parked so he could follow her inside for a closer look.

"I'll take a dozen glazed and a dozen jelly filled, please. Oh and a low fat mocha. Have to watch my weight," she ordered.

Watch your weight go up? the clerk asked in her mind but her mouth said, "Coming right up."

"Hello," Prince greeted when the large, young woman turned. She was a pretty, big girl who looked to be twenty at best.

"Hey," she said shyly, while inwardly saying, *I wanna give you some of this fat pussy.*

"I would love some of that fat pussy," he leaned in and whispered. Her whole body shook as she giggled and blushed. She then mentally revealed that she was a virgin and he really got excited. Not to fuck her but to drink her blood. Virgin blood is always the best.

"Okay," she giggled and shook some more. Prince paid for her donuts and led her away. The Lexus leaned a little when she got in but that only made right turns a little easier as he rushed to get her home. She had eaten the dozen jelly donuts and was halfway into the glaze by the time they reached his block.

Prince scanned the block to make sure the coast was clear before he brought his victims inside. The coast was clear, so he helped hoist the big girl from the small seat.

"Shit!" Prince fussed when his neighbor's door opened and the church lady stepped outside. She was always looking and watching, so he made sure to avoid her. Until tonight as bad timing forced them together.

"Cynthia? Girl, how are you?" she greeted warmly. "How's yo' mama?"

"Fine, they fine," she said and hugged her neck. There was no way Prince could feed off the girl now since there was a witness to say where she was last.

"Oh well," Prince shrugged when they broke off their greeting. He had no choice, so he took her inside and fucked her. Quite a few times actually. Fucked her all night long then, drank from his plasma supply after dropping her off before dawn. The life of a vampire.

******

"Check this out!" Meech sang happily when Prince arrived at the studio.

"Okay," he said and squinted skeptically at the drape covering the vocal booth. He didn't need x-ray vision to guess who was behind it.

"Hit it," Meech told Adam. Adam paused so Meech understood that he didn't work for him. The song was dope though, so he did hit it.

"Okay!" Prince smiled and nodded as the three-part harmony filled the room and beyond. Soulful singing that resonated deep within him. One of the three parts took him back sixty years to when he sang in the choir. She sounded so much like Sister Clara it made his loins jump.

"Un huh! You like! It's dope!" Meech celebrated. Adam nodded too and no one could deny that the song was a hit.

"Yeah, it's dope. Sup with the curtain, though?" Prince conceded and asked as if he didn't know. Again, he asked himself just how ugly can they be. He got a hint when Adam suddenly put his sunglasses on as Meech went for the drapes.

"Ta-dah!" he announced with great fanfare and pulled the drapes away. Keli, Kamala and Tosha stood nervously and awaited another dose of disappointment. The girls knew they could sing but couldn't help how they looked. Actually they could but couldn't actually afford it.

"Beautiful! Just beautiful!" Prince said and gave a slow applause.

"Them!" both Meech and Adam asked incredulously.

"Wus?" bucktooth Keli asked since that was a first.

"He means our singing," Kamala sighed sadly and covered the whole room with her crossed eyes.

"I mean both!" Prince said as they came out of the booth. Tosha smiled so hard, pus oozed from a fresh pimple. "In fact, not only are you guys going on my album. I'm signing you to my imprint!"

"Imprint?" Meech reeled since this was news to him. It shouldn't be since every artist starts his own label once he blows up. Prince hadn't even dropped yet but there was no doubt he was going to blow up. His was a matter of when, not if.

"Dark Prince records," Prince informed. He didn't just plan on being a star, he wanted to own the galaxy.

"Okay!" the girls sang and bounced around. Prince watched their lady parts jiggle as they celebrated. He didn't need to read their minds to know that each one of them wanted to fuck him. He nodded his head since he wanted to fuck them back. In fact, he had big plans for the throwaway girls that no one wanted.

*****

"We finna kill this shit!" Dirt proclaimed backstage. Tonight was the debut of his track with Prince in front of a huge crowd. The city's DJs all had the track and it would be in heavy rotation by the morning.

"Atlanta first, then the world!" Prince repeated. It had become his mantra as of late. He had plans and they all began tonight. He and Meech gave a nod as Dirt was introduced. Dirt Jones put on a typical Dirt Jones show. High energy with his usual theatrics. He rapped, sang and even twerked a little since this was Atlanta.

"Now, I'm finna show y'all the next nigga to blow! Skraight 'offa Dirty records! Y'all put y'all mutha fucking hands up for The Dark Prince!" Dirt announced. He realized his mistake a few seconds later.

Prince came out crooning for the ladies. They screamed, cheered, and made it rain panties on the stage. He switched it up and began to rap like no one has really rapped before. Being the benefactor of so many places, and so many styles, over so many years came pouring into the microphone.

Uh oh, Dirt thought when the DJ threw on the song they recorded together. He was clearly out of his league and knew he had no
business on the same stage with the man. The contrast was clear
when they rapped to the same beat. By the end of their song, his services were no longer needed.

"Fuck!" Matt admitted when he realized what just happened.
He had a feeling this could happen, expected it would happen, and
planned for it. He made a quick call and said, "It's a go!"

Meanwhile, Prince was showing off his stamina for the ladies and
rapped a hundred miles a minute for ten minutes straight. A strange
feeling stopped him mid-rhyme and stole his whole attention. A feeling he hadn't felt in decades. There was a vampire in the house.

"Thanks for coming out!" Prince yelled over the thunderous applause and screams for more. "The album drops next Tuesday! After
party is at the W hotel!"

"After party?" Meech asked when Prince returned from the stage.

"Small gathering. I got it," he said since he read that Meech wanted to get home to his family.

"You got it? You sure? Cuz I'll come and—"

"Nah, I got it," Prince assured him since the invitation was strictly
for the vampire in attendance.

"Okay then. I'll just go on home. See what my shawty up to,"
Meech said.

"Good idea," Prince nodded. If something was missing from his
life, it was a shawty of his own. He liked Meech because Meech had
a good heart. Opposites attract because Prince did not.

CHAPTER 5

"Really?" Prince sighed when he saw two men lurking near his car as he left the club through the back entrance. He didn't need to read minds to figure out that they were up to no good. He did anyway to find out exactly what.

"Is that right?" he giggled at their plans and walked right by them. They had their orders but were helpless against Prince's mind control. He hopped in his car and rolled off just as Dirt and Matt came out.

'The fuck?' Matt wondered as he watched the target just roll away unscathed.

"He ain't all that!" Dirt said to make himself feel better after being shown up at his own show. "I mean, he okay, but he can't twerk!"

"Nah," Matt said as his shooters made their way over. He wanted a reason why they just let Prince go. He got it when they both raised their guns and gunned Dirt down right next to him.

"Not him! What the fuck are you knuckle heads doing!" he shouted over the shots.

"I'on know," one of the shooters replied since the spell wore off after they carried out their commands. Matt could only shake his head as his meal ticket bled out on the ground. The shooters ran off once the deed was done.

"Guess I'll slide up under Prince," Matt said and nodded in agreement. It could work since Prince kept his friends close and his food even closer. He had a date with a crematorium and didn't even know it.

Prince rode over to the W hotel and entered the bar. He amused himself watching the flock of birds trying to get past security for the after party that wasn't. The presence of another vampire wiped the smile off his face. He whipped his head around and came face to face with a familiar face.

"I knew it! I knew it! I ain't no vampire! You tripping. Ain't no such thing!" the man laughed as he recounted the excuses Prince gave a decade ago. He had aged those ten years, but Prince recognized him instantly.

"Butta? How you—"

"Became a vampire anyway. Since you wouldn't turn me," he mocked. Prince realized he couldn't get inside the man's head and that spelled danger. The more powerful a vampire is, the less likely to read his thoughts. The power that comes from killing other vampires.

"Yeah," Prince nodded. He knew he couldn't read his mind either but both men knew what was on the other's mind.

"Man, I read every report of bloodless bodies after you left. I chased them around all over until I ended up in Haiti. Met a mutual friend of ours..." he said and trailed off so Prince could finish.

"Katrina! Why did she let you live?" he asked, straining to get inside his mind. He now knew the woman had only turned him to kill him as she had done countless men.

"She had no choice once I put a stake through her heart. We're allergic to that kind of stuff, you know?" he said and smiled. Butta let his fangs slide down and back just to show off.

"So, what are we going to do?" Prince asked and was ready for whatever. Timelines would be flooded with the most fantastic fight footage in history. Two vampires fighting to the death in the W hotel.

"Live in peace or die in conflict?" he asked since those were the choices. "I like you, Prince. We're a lot alike, you and me."

"We rap and drink blood," he agreed and let his claws slowly come out under the table.

"Yeah, but still, there can be only one. Enjoy your career. I'll come through in ten, twenty years and we can see what's up," Butta shrugged.

"We can," Prince said and accepted the challenge. Part of him wanted to attack and settle the matter here and now. That contradicted his plans, so he sat tight. He watched Butta scoop a pretty white woman from the bar and exit the building.

He used a back exit to avoid the birds and headed over to Roshawn's house for dinner and desert. After feeding on the mother, he fed the daughter some dick. Once his hunger and thirst were satisfied, he went home and went to sleep.

"In what Atlanta police are calling are calling the strangest thing they have ever seen..." Prince heard as he half listened to the news. It now had his full attention and he turned the volume up higher than necessary.

"A headless corpse was found in the middle of Piedmont park..." the woman said happily.

"Butta!" Prince said when she reported the head had been found in the lake. He didn't need to be there to know his brother vampire chopped her head off and drank from the fountain of blood pouring from the severed jugulars. Gaping wounds don't leave telltale bite marks that show their hand. His findings were confirmed when a picture of the victim was posted from earlier times. It was the same pretty woman from the bar.

Prince wasn't the only one playing close attention to the headless corpse.

"The vampire lady is here!" the assistant announced when Kristine Musa arrived back at the morgue.

"Yes she is," Kristine said sharply from the last minute flight back to Atlanta. Headless bodies were on the rise so she rushed from Chicago from that one to this one.

"Well, we have a real sicko on our hands but no vampires," the medical examiner said just as sharply. "A white woman was killed and people wanted answers!"

"They can live with the black bodies that filled his morgue but when white people get killed it's a problem!" the clerk shot back.

"Take a knee," the other pathologist quipped to calm the tension. "And yes, Mizz Musa, the body was devoid of body fluids. All that indicates is that this was a secondary crime scene. I will bet dollars to donuts that there's a primary scene somewhere loaded with blood!"

"And you would lose your dollars and your donuts!" she shot back when she saw the unmistakable signs of a vampire. Just the shock alone in the eyes of the head sitting beside the body gave hint of the sheer horror of her last moments.

She wasn't sure if the vampire was from here, or coming here to feed. This was unusually sloppy as of they wanted it to be known. As if someone wanted her to find a vampire so she could destroy it.

"I read you're working on a cure. A serum to turn immortals back to mortals?" the clerk asked eagerly. He was a part-time vampire buff himself and the prospect of that intrigued him.

"Mmhm," was all she cared to say in front of the skeptics. They made a tacit agreement to talk over lunch and she went back to examining the body. By the conclusion, she concluded this was definitely a vampire. "Well. thank you, gentlemen."

"Anytime. Next time we have a vampire," the M.E said sarcastically. Kristine smiled softly at the thought of sending the vampire to his house whenever she caught up with him.

"I guess I'll grab lunch," the clerk said as soon as Kristine cleared the room.

"Because you've worked so hard," the doctor laughed some more. He was on one today, so he just let him have it. He smiled, nodded, and rushed out to catch up with the vampire lady.

*****

"Daniel," the clerk introduced as he sat across from Kristine in the restaurant booth. "And I believe in vampires!"

"You should believe!" Kristine said with enough conviction to make him a believer if he wasn't.

"Are they here? In Atlanta!" he asked wide-eyed with awe.

"It's nothing romantic about vampires! They're monsters, not movies stars or rappers," she fussed and dimmed the star struck light in his eyes. Her warning was wasted on the vampire fanatic.

"But that would be cool, right? A vampire who is like a rapper!" he said with his eyes even wider. Kristine just shook her head and pulled out her photo and pulled up some pictures.

"Look. This is what vampires do!" she said and shoved the phone in his face. His face changed when he saw the woman with her throat bit away. Her spine was visible in the gaping hole. "What, you thought they just make neat little pin holes? No, they're animals. That was my mother. Murdered in her own bed."

"Wow," Daniel exclaimed when the gory picture made him grab it.

"She met him in a bar and took him home. He took what she gave him, then took her life," she said. Her native British accent came to the front as she reminisced.

"So, they said you were working on a cure?" he asked as his fascination came back.

"Cure or a kill? Vampires are a virus, a cancer. I'm close. Just not easy tracking them down. I'm all over the globe every time I get a report."

"So, do you really think there's a vampire in Atlanta?" he asked as his eyes went wide once more.

"I don't know. I do know the two victims I've seen are vampire attacks. I'm sure of that."

"Not to mention all the missing people. People just disappearing off the face of the earth," Daniel added. Some were runaways while others ended up in Prince's crematorium. He used their ashes as kitty litter for his black cats.

"Well, here's my number. I want you to stay vigilant. Call me the moment you hear or see anything," Kristine said and handed him her card.

"Or I could call you to hang out sometimes," he suggested. It was only right because she was a beautiful woman with a naked ring finger.

"Or not," she said with a flattered smile. Her busy life left no room for a love life. The smile dissipated just as quick and she added. "Stay on point. There very well may be a vampire in Atlanta!"

CHAPTER 6

"That's crazy!" Meech repeated as his head kept shaking. It began moving from side to side when the news of Dirt's murder reached him.

"Yeah, I'on know why someone would want to kill him!" Matt moaned. He came straight to room B the next night looking for the next coattail to ride. Next jock strap to swing from.

"Sup," Prince asked as he arrived and cracked a brand new smile.

"Yoooo! Them shits is dope!" Meech cheered and came closer to inspect his new platinum and diamond fangs.

"Bruh..." Prince laughed and leaned back when he got a little too close for comfort. They were dope and fully functional, and super sharp.

"Those are fiyah!" Matt added. He knew his survival depended upon him getting in good with Prince since Dirt was no more.

"Mmhm. Why are you here?" Prince asked as if he didn't already know. He wanted to get the man's mind churning so he could extract his next move.

"Dirt got kilt after y'all show last night!" Meech answered for him. "Shoot, I need to go tell my grandma. And all Dirk's baby mamas."

"Go handle your business," Prince advised. The album was done, so he really wasn't needed anyway.

"Okay. Yeah," Meech agreed and took off leaving Matt and Prince alone.

"Looks like just you and me," Prince said and listened in.

Man I hope this nigga ain't gay! Matt thought. *I guess I could blow him, if I had to? Just real quick, get it over with.*

"Nothing like that. I'm definitely not gay," Prince laughed. He laughed even harder at the confused look on his face.

"I, my bad, I..." he stammered. Matt assumed he thought out loud.

"I know what you did. With Dirt," he whispered even though they were alone.

"Me? Nah I, and we, Un-uh!" he said, shaking his head.

"Sure you did. They were supposed to get me, but I changed their minds. Just like I'm going to change yours," Prince laughed and stood. He said the rest into the man's mind and left the room. Prince had a triple date all to himself.

"Man," Matt moaned as he set off to do something he really didn't want to do. He was unable to stop himself as his body complied to the instructions planted in his head. He took the elevator to the roof and promptly walked right off the edge. He landed right on his head and joined his boss down at the morgue.

"Tragic!" Prince laughed at the thud sound he heard as he pulled out of the parking lot.

*****

A few miles and minutes later, he arrived at the upscale restaurant for his date. He smiled at the commotion out front, knowing it only helped his cause. He chose the beautiful spot, filled with beautiful people for a reason.

"We wat weservations!" the bucktoothed third of Prince's new group protested when the maitre D refused to let them in.

"It's cuz we ugly? Huh!" Tosha said and scratched a bloody bump. The man grimaced at the gruesome girls and held firm.

"I see how you are!" cross-eyed Kamala nodded and looked in all directions. One of her eyes spotted Prince as he pulled up. "Tell this man we supposed to be here!"

"They are supposed to be here," he repeated when he arrived on scene. The snobby little fellow immediately stepped aside so they could enter.

"Enjoy your meal, ladies," he said with a curtsy. The girls frowned in confusion at the sudden change in his mean demeanor.

"Dang!" Kamala cheered at the juice Prince had, then again when she looked around the swanky restaurant. "Dang!"

"Thwis pwace wocks!" Keli proclaimed. Heads turned to see the handsome man and odd-looking girls as they were led to their reserved table. Prince walked with his head high as if he had the baddest chicks in the city. Actually he did, once he brought it out of them.

"Here you are. Can I get you any drinks before your meal?" The hostess asked once they were seated.

"Dom P," he said, causing the deprived girls to giggle. They had heard of Dom Perignom before but never actually had any. A few minutes later, the waitress arrived and began to pour.

"Ladies," she said but didn't get to the gentleman.

"None for me. I'm driving," Prince said and declined. He smiled softly at the thoughts bouncing around in the girls heads. They all wanted to fuck him and he wanted to fuck them back. They waited and looked around in amazement for their food to come so they could say they actually ate here.

"What you want with us?" Tosha wanted to know.

"It's not what I want. It's what I can give you girls," he corrected. "Now, what do you want?"

"I want to be was stwar!" Keli announced triumphantly.

"And what would you do to become a star?" he asked and peered into her soul. Perhaps a little too deep because she got stuck and couldn't answer.

"Look, mister. You know how many dudes said they could do something with us just to get some pussy? I even gave a couple of them what they wanted and still ain't get no dang where!" Kamala fussed. She still wanted to fuck him, just without all the games.

"Word!" Tosha cosigned. There was a brief pause when the waitress returned with the biggest steaks the girls had ever seen.

"None for you?" she asked once more before departing.

"None for me," Prince said as he watched his meals enjoy their meal. He waited until between dinner and desert before making his pitch. "I can give you want you want."

"And just what do we want?" Kamala demanded.

"Fame. Fortune. Riches beyond your wildest dreams..."

"I hwave some pwetty wild dweams!" Keli confessed.

"You do," Prince agreed since she was daydreaming about riding his face backwards while she ate. "But I can deliver. I got next and you know it."

"He do got next!" Tosha agreed. "So, what we gotta do? What you want from us? Sex?"

"Of course I want sex, but you want that, too. We can go fuck and then you all can go back to your mundane lives. Or..." he said and let them take the lead.

"Or what?" they asked in the perfect harmony that would make them stars.

"Give yourselves to me. Body, mind and soul," he replied. He wouldn't use his mind control since this had to be with their free will.

"Okay!" they all agreed. The desert arrived and all three took a bite.

"Save some room for the dick," Prince reminded since the night was young. He cracked up when all three spit their cake back on the plate and pushed them away. "Check please!"

*****

"This is okay," Kamala announced when they reached his westside home. It was nice, clean and a hell of a lot better than her rundown apartments. She just expected so much more for the man who just promised them the whole world.

"Yes. It's my family home. I was born here," he said as he led them inside.

"Well, I like it!" Tosha said and shot her a stern glance that said, "don't fuck this up".

"Me twoo!" Keli proclaimed and shot her friend the same look. She wanted it all too but right now, she wanted some dick. She didn't get much dick since she looked so funny.

Prince still planned to fuck them and led them straight to his bedroom. Once they arrived, he began to strip. The girls intended to strip as well, but got stuck by the beautiful, black, naked man with a big, beautiful, black dick.

"Care to join me?" he asked once he was naked.

"How you 'sposed to do it to all of us at the same time?" Kamala wanted to know. Meanwhile, Keli and Tosha raced to get naked with him.

"Like this..." Prince said and got down to work. He picked Keli up and gently placed her on his tongue so she could ride his face backwards. She leaned forward and showed how her teeth got bucked. First, she sucked her thumb as a child but now the curve of her teeth was perfect to work a dick.

"Let me," Tosha said and pushed her friend away. Keli got caught up with the tongue circling her clit and braced herself. Prince reached over and fingered Kamala's pussy until she bust a nut all over his fingers.

"I'm fwinna cwome!" Keli announced and did just that. She tipped over and curled up into a fetal ball as she shivered and shook from her first orgasm. He pulled Tosha up to mount his mouth while Kamala threw her leg over his waist so she could ride the dick.

It may have been three against one but that wasn't enough. Prince fucked those girls every which way humanly possible. Each had so many orgasms they were dehydrated from losing so much liquid.

"No more!" Kamala pleaded and tapped out. She joined her friends curled up in the corner.

"Now, are you ready to give yourselves to me?" Prince asked in a tone that made them rise.

"Yes," they sang and nodded. Prince smiled and let his long fangs slide out. Each had a chance to decline but neither did. Instead, they all lifted their heads up and back to show their pretty necks.

Prince licked Kamala's thick jugular vein and felt the blood coursing through it. He slowly sank his fangs inside and felt her knees buckle below. He held her in place and drank until her pulse began to slow.

Keli practically shoved Keli aside so she could go next. She was next and he drank from her neck until she was weak. He laid her next to one friend and did the same to the other friend.

The three girls were weak from loss of blood but still watched as Prince used his claw to open his wrist. There were three girls and on-ly two wrists, so he made an incision in the thick, curly vein that ran the length of his dick. This allowed all three to drink of his blood at the same time. The wounds closed immediately once the feeding was over.

"Time to die, ladies. I'll see you when you awake."

CHAPTER 7

"Man, I can't get hold to the girls! I called Kamala all night and she won't answer. Tosha going straight to voicemail and Keli ain't got no phone!" Meech said, sounding like worry wart.

"I heard from them. Matter fact, I sent them down to Mexico. To get some work done," Prince explained which would explain how they would look the next time they were seen.

"Mexico? Work? What kinda work?" he questioned but wasn't getting any answers.

"We ready for next Tuesday?" Prince asked since it was his release date. By next Wednesday, Dark Prince would be a household name. They released the single with him and Dirt and it was blowing up the charts. The world wanted to know of he could hold his own for sixteen tracks. The only thing left was to shoot the video so the world could get a glimpse of him.

"Oh yeah!" we booked the hottest club in the city!" Meech cheered. It was debatable since there were plenty of hot clubs in the city of Atlanta. He chose this one to show how much the tables had turned. Now those same bouncers who turned their noses up at him would have to cater to him. Prince cracked a smirk at the thought since his friend deserved it.

"How was the service?" Prince managed to ask without laughing. Today was the day they put Dirt in the dirt and he found it quite amusing.

"Crazy. His baby mamas lost their damn minds!" Meech laughed and filled him in on the theatrics. His mood got somber when it came time to talk business. "Only thing, with Dirt dead we ain't got the bread for the video shoot. And we running out of time."

"Set it up. I'll go to the bank tomorrow and get it," Prince said, solving the dilemma.

"A hundred grand! Just go to the bank and get a hundred grand?" Meech asked incredulously.

"Should I get two?" he asked since money was no object. All he needed to do was ask the manager to transfer money into his account. When you have the power of hypnosis, people do what you tell them. "Yeah, I'll just have two."

*****

Kristine Musa didn't have the power of hypnosis but she had a super power of her own. She couldn't leap a tall building in a single bound, but she had a walk on her that turned heads so hard, some men got whiplash. Besides her brain, her big ass was her biggest asset. It wiggled like a worm on a hook and her prey always took the bait.

Excuse me, miss," a debonair Latino gentleman greeted when he approached her in the Bahamian night club. Reports of bloodless bodies caught her ear and here she was.

"American?" she asked in mock shock. He thought he was randomly selecting her but it was she who selected him.

"Yes. California!" he smiled and sat down. "I'm Pablo. Born in Mexico but been in Los Angeles for a lifetime."

"At least," she smiled back at her own wordplay. Pablo had been in Los Angeles for a couple of lifetimes since he was three hundred years old. He had a pattern of island hopping to feed. A pattern picked up on by a very smart vampire hunter. He had a type, so she became it. The timing was perfect and in inhaled the sweet scent of her menstrual cycle.

"Would you like to go somewhere quiet and talk?" Pablo asked as he listened to her heartbeat though her chest.

"No, I would rather go somewhere and fuck loudly. I have a suite," she said and instantly shut her thoughts down. She didn't know if he could read minds or not so she kept hers blank. She blinked twice and went totally blonde.

"I have a villa! We can—" he began, but didn't end.

"I prefer my own place," Kristine said and stood. Pablo looked her up and down and forget all about his villa. She knew when he would follow when she walked away. A short walk later, they reached her beachfront bungalow. It was right on the beach to capture the brilliant Caribbean sunrise.

"Nice. Not as nice as my villa, but it'll do," Pablo quipped as they entered. He shrugged and remembered why they were there.

"I have my cycle. Lay down while I shower," she announced. She stepped out of her dress to show what she was working with.

"I don't mind blood. In fact, I prefer it," Pablo said and came out of his clothes as he came near. He scooped her off her feet and laid her down on the large four-poster bed. The handcuffs on the headboard spelled out, "F.R.E.A.K."

"On your back!" she demanded and went to remove his dick.

"Okay then!" he said and complied. She immediately strapped his wrist to the ornate headboard. He felt strange the moment she did. "I feel..."

"Weak?" she asked as she rolled off the bed and covered herself. "Your laying on sheets infused with pure silver."

"Let me up!" Pablo screamed, hissed, and bared his fangs. It would have been scary to most people but Kristine Musa wasn't most people. She was a vampire hunter and knew she was in control. The sheets and cuffs were made from vampire kryptonite pure silver. It sapped his strength from the moment it touched him. He wouldn't die but got weaker by the second.

"What is that?" Pablo demanded when Kristine began to draw a bright green fluid up into a syringe.

"It doesn't actually have a name. Been so busy trying to make sure it works," she admitted as she checked the amount. She scrunched her face and added a little more.

"What am I, your guinea pig?" he complained as she came over with the needle.

"I actually had a guinea pig once. It died," she admitted and inserted the needle.

"What does this do?" Pablo asked as he felt the liquid spreading throughout his body.

"It reverses the virus. Supposed to anyway. It worked once. Well, kind of. It cured the fellow but he aged a thousand years in two minutes and turned to dust," she sighed.

"Did you just shrug? You can't just shrug after turning someone into dust!" he moaned.

"You feed on people! Then toss them aside like trash! So..." she snapped and shrugged again to spite him. The conversation came to an end as the concoction began to work. Kristine was hopeful when his fangs and claws slowly retracted.

"I th—think it—it's working?" Pablo asked as he began to feel more human than he had in three hundred years.

"We're about to see..." Kristine said as the pink predawn glow lined the horizon. She opened the drapes and watched as the true dawn began to spread.

"I'm cured!" Pablo cheered when the direct sunlight didn't burn.

"Uh oh..." she moaned a minute later when he began to smoke and sizzle.

She could have closed the curtains and tried again but didn't. She shrugged once more and went back to the drawing board. Pablo growled and howled as the fire consumed him. It wasn't a total failure and she was getting closer. Now she just needed another vampire to experiment on. Luckily for her, new vampires were made everyday.

*****

"They should be about ripe now," Prince said and went to check on his princesses. He put the dead girls in the guest room while awaiting them to become undead. "Ah yes!"

"I feel so different," Keli said. She noticed the change in her speech and ran her tongue over her now perfectly straight teeth. She smiled wider and brighter than ever before.

"Me, too," Tosha said and touched her face. It was once as bumpy as a topographic globe, but was now as smooth as a baby's bottom.

"I can see!" Kamala said as her vision was clear. She had almost become used to the doubled vision of her wandering eyes. Now, they were straight and focused.

"Look," Prince said and pointed to a full length mirror on the closet door.

The girls rushed over and marveled at their new selves. The jock-eyed for position in front of the mirror. They looked the same, but different. Not only had their afflictions been fixed but booties were rounder and breast were fuller. Stomachs were flatter, faces were clear, eyes, and teeth were straight.

"We fine as hell!" Kalama shouted after checking herself and her friends out.

"Yes, you are," Prince agreed. He stepped aside and parted the blackout curtains. Just enough to let in enough sunlight to make his point.

"Ahhh!" Keli screamed when the UV rays touched her arm. Nothing gets a point across more effectively than some heat. She pulled away when her skin blistered and sizzled.

"You are now creatures of the night," he began and laid out the do's and don'ts of their new lifestyle. Not all of them of course just in case he had to use them on them and make sure they could never use them on him.

"So!" Tosha shouted defiantly as she checked herself out once again. No one had ever called her pretty before, but now everyone would. She was their leader and Prince already knew how that would eventually end.

"We need new clothes!" Keli said since her old clothes were no match for her new body.

"Look at my titties!" Kamala said as she admired the plump, heavy breast in the mirror once more.

"Actually, I would like to do a lot more than just look," Prince said and took one of her brown nipples into his mouth. His dick stood straight out but luckily, Tosha was right there. She opened wide and gave him a warm welcome inside of her mouth.

The rest of the afternoon was spent in a three-way fuck-fest. Prince had the stamina to go all day but now the girls did too. There was no clear winner by the time the sun began it's descent to the west. Prince knew one day it would rise from that direction. Until then, he would rule the night.

*****

"Wow!" Keli sang as the team entered the mall. She stared up and down and all around like she'd never step foot in the place ever in life.

"You act like you ain't never been here before!" Tosha fussed.

"Not shopping!" she declared. "And look at errbody looking at us!"

"Cuz, look at us!" Kamala shouted and pointed at their reflections in the mirror.

"The hottest new girl group in the world!" Prince explained. The once shy girls lifted their heads triumphantly and literally bought the mall out. Prince spent thousands of dollars on his girls to get them ready for the video shoot and the world.

"Why I ain't hungry?" Tosha asked as they traveled through the food court, loaded down with bags.

"Me either!" Keli and Kamala sang like backup.

"You will be," Prince laughed. He was feeling the pangs of thirst and knew they would too. When they did, it would be feeding time.

"Sup, shawty? Hey, lil' mama!" the spokesman for a group of guys called when the girls passed by there table. They saw Prince was clearly with them but kids today don't have much respect for much.

"Man, fuck them bitches!" another one snarled. Tosha stopped in her tracks upon hearing the insult. She'd been called a bitch by her mother for as long as she could remember. She couldn't do anything about it then but knew she could now. She looked at Prince for approval and got it with a nod.

"Sup, playboy. What y'all tryna get into?" Tosha asked seductively as she approached the table.

"Shit, we tryna get into you!" the spokesman declared. "And her and her!"

"Let's ride then," she offered and turned away, knowing they would follow. Follow they did like sheep to slaughter. "I'm fixing to ride with them."

"See you at the house," Prince said as Kamala took the spot she vacated by their side. There was a definitive pecking order amongst his hens and Keli was in the rear. Tosha was a big yellow girl, while Kamala was a little browner and smaller. Keli was a jet black, petite thing with ass and titties for days.

Tosha endured getting felt up along with the crude remarks of the guys as they rode over to Prince's westside home. Her thirst built slowly and steadily from the sound of the four heartbeats, beating loudly in the car. She could hear it over their boisterous banter and bass beating through the stereo system.

"Pull behind the Lexus," she directed when they reached the house.

"Your girls in here, too?" one of the backseat passengers asked hopefully. He didn't mind running a train on her but his stature in the crew meant a messy fourth in line for the vagina.

"The whole gang is here!" she sang and lured them inside with her swaying hips. Straight up the stairs into the spare room used for feeding. Prince dubbed it the "Boom-boom room" and had it lined with nonporous surfaces for easy cleanup. Keli and Kamala awaited nakedly inside

"What he doing here?" the spokesman demanded when they reached the boom boom room and saw Prince there as well. To make matters worse he was as naked as the girls were.

"You're probably not going to like the answer," Prince laughed. He laughed even harder at the looks on their faces when his erection grew right before their eyes.

"I ain't with this!" one of the dudes protested. He turned to leave but Keli moved like a black blur and blocked the door.

"Move out my way, bitch!" another demanded and moved in to move her. He sounded real tough until she bared her fangs and hissed loudly. Now he sounded like a damsel in distress and tried to run.

Prince fell back like a lion king and let his lionesses hunt. Tosha took the lead and took their leader by his throat. She lifted him off the floor with his feet dangling in the air.

"Didn't you say you wanted me to go down on you?" she reminded of the crude remarks on the ride over. He threatened to fuck her face and come down her throat, but only shook his head as she dipped low. Her mouth opened wide and engulfed his entire package that had shriveled from sheer fear. It's unclear if he or his friends screamed louder when she bit his junk off and spit it aside. She opened wide and let the waterfall of blood fall into her mouth.

His friends were still howling and fighting to get through the door. They would have to get through Keli first but Keli was thirsty. She went straight for a jugular and clamped her fangs down. She wrapped her arms and legs around the flailing man and drank. She drank like a Bedouin who found an oasis after a week of travel.

Kamala attacked a third man from the rear. She bit through his spine and left him in a paralyzed heap on the floor. She went down with him and fed. The last man made a Superman worthy leap for the window. It probably would have been quite impressive had Prince not grabbed his ankle and snatched him right out of the air. He slung him back inside and watched as all three moved in for the kill.

"Save me some," he laughed as the greedy girls all drank from different parts of the last man. They didn't but he didn't mind, he had plenty of plasma to drink. Once the feeding frenzy was complete they had an orgy right there in the bloody room.

CHAPTER 8

"Still ain't heard from the girls! My bad. I ain't know you had company," Meech said nervously as he entered Prince's trailer at the video shoot. The girls giggled and made him do a double take. "Tosha? Kamala? Keli?"

"Better known as Princesses!" Tosha informed. They all got a good laugh as he blinked in disbelief at the transformation. Prince really got a kick out of the thoughts running through his mind as he looked over the girls and their new look.

I could have hit that, he thought of Tosha and turned to Kamala, *I should have hit that,* then Keli got a *I still might hit that!* Nah, Angela gone whip my ass if I did. Shoot, I need to send Angela to Mexico, too!'

"They ready? We ready," Prince announced and pulled Meech from his hilarious thoughts.

She ready alright! he thought once more, taking another look at the plump camel toe protruding between Tosha's legs. *Bet that's some good pussy!*

"It is. Especially when it get to talking back," Prince laughed again.

Meech cocked his head curiously when Prince revealed what he was thinking. He was sure he hadn't blurted it out, so he wondered how did he know. Prince read those thoughts too and steered the conversation in another direction.

"We gone shoot this video or not? We don't have all night."

"Fah sho! Angela came to watch, too!" Meech said excitedly. Prince got the rest out of his mind and offered to put her in a scene.

"She can be an extra," he suggested, causing Meech to smile broadly. "I would love to meet her."

"She wanna meet you, too!" he gushed as they stepped out of the trailer. He looked around and spotted his woman talking to her old boss. She told some of her ex-coworkers about the video shoot and they came out to see for themselves.

"Hey!" Angela cheesed widely when Meech bought their meal ticket over to meet her. Her life had changed for the better thanks to the handsome man in front of her.

"Hello, yourself. I've heard a lot about you," Prince greeted and shook her hand. His smile was genuine when she lowered her head and giggled shyly. Not a single impure thought crossed her mind as they shook hands. He heard something inside of her and accidentally let the cat out of the bag. "Congratulations on your pregnancy!"

"Pregnancy! You pregnant?" Meech reeled since she hadn't told him yet. She just found out herself but Prince heard the second heart beating inside of her when their hands touched.

"Yup! Congrats! You finna be a daddy again!" Angela cheered. This wasn't how she planned to tell him but it was out now. Almost all faces smiled happily except for her old boss. Prince didn't need to go inside Jeff's head since the malice was clear on his face.

Woulda been my baby if she kept working with me. Already had her jacking my dick for extra hours, he thought while the couple shared a special moment. Prince leaned over and shared a special moment with Tosha. She smiled, nodded, and plotted. Once the niceties were out of the way, they got down to the business of shooting the video.

"I'm hungry!" Keli pouted halfway through the shoot. Her fangs began to slowly come down as she eyed all the food dancing and gyrating all over the room.

"Control yourself!" Prince growled. New vampires always had to learn self-restraint being in a room full of warm bodies threatened to get the best of her.

"I'm trying, but I'm hungry," she groaned. Prince pulled her by the hand into the trailer. He made sure to bring packets of plasma along just in case. She devoured the first one and was halfway through the next while Prince just shook his head. He knew then, this one could be a problem.

Most videos shoot all day and into the night. This one shot all night and wrapped up just before dawn. Luckily, the director got all he needed by the time Prince and the Princesses abruptly departed.

Tosha didn't ride with the rest since she and Jeff were hitting it off so good. She offered to ride his dick, so he offered to give her a ride home. They arrived shortly after Prince and the other girls. She took him straight up to the "Boom boom room" and devoured him.

*****

The first song featured the girls and would be their introduction to world, as well. The next night they would be in the studio recording their first album. Writing and producing their entire project on their own meant they would soon all be millionaires. The would have to get it recorded.

"Keli?" Prince said when he saw Keli staring at Adam's Adams Apple as he mixed their song.

"I'm hungry," she pouted. Some vampires have a thirst that can never be quenched and she was one of them. Being in close quarters with a warm blooded mortal was driving her crazy. She could hear his heartbeat thundering over the music.

"I got what I need!" Adam announced once he checked the playback. Being well prepared allowed the girls to record several songs each session and the bulk of their debut project was complete. All that was left was the mixing and mastering.

"Good! Let's go grab a bite to eat," Prince suggested and stood. Kamala nearly bared her fangs at the mention of food. Instead, she smiled at his offhanded word play.

"A bite, huh?" she laughed and stood with him. Keli stood and Adam checked out her curvy curves up close. They had been staring at each other all night but for different reasons. He wanted to fuck her while she wanted to drain every drop of blood from his body. A relationship like that would never last.

"Say uh, Keli. Wanna hang out for a while?" Adam asked before she could get away.

"Yes!" she practically cheered but Prince shot them both down.

"No! She's with me! They're all with me!" he said forcefully but only because he liked the guy.

"Okay, my bad!" Adam said and raised his hands in surrender. He called him a greedy muthafucka in head since he was hording the booty.

"I'll be that." Prince replied. He liked Adam plus he was a dope engineer so he didn't want to eat him.

"Catch you later," Keli said and licked her tongue at him on the way out.

"I have a wonderful meal for all of us," Prince said once they got underway. He had Roshawn meet him at a location he wouldn't be at so she wouldn't be home when he arrived with his greedy girls.

"Enough for all of us?" Keli asked and squinted skeptically. She got her answer a few minutes later when Prince let them inside. Roshawn had given him a key so he could help himself to her vagina anytime he wanted. Once again, that good vagina saved her life and Prince sent her on an empty mission. He planned to get her a place downtown anyway since her home was about to be a crime scene once again.

"Hello, Mr. Prince," Roshawn's mother huffed when he entered her room. She began to spread her big legs so he could eat, until she saw the Princesses entered behind him.

Keli bared her fangs and flew across the room in a blur. The large women let out a gurgled groan when she slammed her teeth into her. Kamala cut off her screams when she latched on to her neck. Tosha took the other side and began to feed.

Prince lifted a meaty arm and bit away a mound of fat to get to her artery. Animalistic grunts and growls filled the room as the three vampires fed. He was right and the large woman was enough to satisfy their communal thirst. More than enough, but Roshawn returned to retrieve her phone.

"Hey, mama. I—" she began when she walked in on four vampires feeding on her mother.

"No!" Prince shouted when Keli attacked. She stopped but had already taken a bite out of her neck. A burst of blood skeeted from the gaping hole where her jugular vein once was.

Kamala couldn't ignore the flow of fresh blood and rushed over to clamp her mouth over the gusher. He could only shake his head as he watched his favorite sex toy eaten alive.

"You're going to take up her slack!" Prince fussed towards Keli.

"My pleasure!" she said and smiled with the blood version of a milk mustache.

*****

"You ready, my nigga? This is it! We big time now!" Meech was hyped backstage as Prince prepared for his album release party.

"Yup," he shot back casually. Meech was right about the big time since the touring company just cut a check for a five million dollar advance. A drop in the bucket compared to what was coming once they hit the road.

Meech's share was a cool million and he bought a house for his family. He bought new cars for himself, Angela, and one for his grandmother. Prince spent a little money too and bought a condo downtown to be close to the action. He couldn't move in just yet since his Princesses couldn't be left alone.

The girls first single featuring Prince shot to number two on the top eight at eight. The only thing stopping them from the number one spot was Prince. The takeover had officially begun.

"Okay, the girls gonna warm em up! You knock em out!" Meech said when the DJ announced the show. He rushed to take his rightful place in the VIP so he could watch the show.

The packed crowd was made up of hip hop heads from all walks of life. There were thots and thugs mingling with students destined to be doctors and lawyers. Including one future medical examiner front and center stage.

"Mmm!" Daniel grunted when Princesses took the stage. All three wore very little and showed off a whole lot.

Tosha wore a tiny pair of shorts pulled so snugly into her crotch, it made a perfect imprint of the fat camel toe beneath. Kamala took it a step further in a sheer body suit that shows her entire body. Keli, bless her heart, wore a mini dress short enough to show her freshly shaved box. And they could sing!

Daniel was just one of many fans aiming their camera phones at the stage. His like many men got plenty of footage up Keli's dress as she sang and twerked on the stage.

Their last song was the song they recorded with Prince. He began rapping offstage to build the hype. The crowd was in a frenzy, then exploded with cheers as he came out. His appearance was nothing short of magnificent and mesmerizing. Men and women both stared up in awe as he rapped. The platinum and diamond fangs glistened in brilliant flashes when he opened his mouth.

No one noticed when the Princesses exited the stage since Prince had their full attention. Meanwhile, Keli had caught the attention of an iced out patron. His money and rep got him backstage to mingle with performers. He picked Keli out the crew and made his move.

"Sup, shawty. You look good out there," he said and smiled to show off his own white gold fangs. He ran his eyes all over her body like one does a piece of meat at the butcher shop.

"You look good back here," she said, giving him the same looks he was giving her.

"You looking like you tryna do something," he dared.

"I am!" Keli said eagerly. The man pulled her by her hand and out the side door. He fumbled with a key fob and unlocked his tricked out truck.

"Come on!" he urged and pulled her up into the back seat. A lot of dudes swear they don't eat pussy and they would be lying. He dove face first and splashed between her legs and lapped at her labia.

"You go boy!" she cheered as he expertly ate her out. She pulled her legs up and put her feet on the headliner. He did go and she came in his mouth moments later.

"My tur—" he began with his lips glistening like a glazed donut. The sight of her fangs stopped his request right in his throat. He was about to ask for some head but changed his mind when he saw her fangs.

"No, it's still my turn!" she said and attacked his jugular. He struggled, punched, and kicked but couldn't detach the woman from his neck. The struggle caused his heart to beat faster and blood gushed into her mouth. He grew weaker with every swallow until he had nothing left.

Keli wiped her mouth and eased back inside the club just before Prince wrapped up his set onstage. Kamala did a double take when she slid next to her. She thought she smelled fresh blood but didn't see anything out of the usual.

"Thank you!" Prince concluded and gave a humble bow. He knew he just killed the shit and the shower of panties only proved it. A last scan of the crowd brought him face to face with Daniel's camera before he exited the stage.

"Can we go eat now?" Tosha purred seductively. Food always made them amorous and she was ready to fuck him after that performance. She wasn't the only one.

"Y'all hoes can't come back here!" a burley security guard fussed at a group of girls who tried to get back stage.

"Let them through," Prince directed since he could literally smell their licentiousness on their breath. One was on her cycle and the vampires picked that up too.

The blood of the pure was always best but he preferred to feed on the bad. Just one of the many lessons he learned from Katrina. She fed off the people less likely to be missed. The ones no one would be shocked when they went missing. That's why she was able to survive as long as she did. His mind shifted to Butta and his claims of killing her. Katrina was strong, so he would have to be even stronger. He avoided other vampires to avoid the unavoidable battle to the death. Still he knew he and Butta would eventually butt heads.

"We loved y'all show!" the leader of the pack of hood rats declared when she reached the group. She liked pussy as much as dick so she courted him and them. It didn't matter which way she went since she went both ways.

"I like her!" Tosha declared. "Can I have her?"

"We can share her. We can share them all!" Prince said. The large group made it over to Prince's house and up the stairs. Keli and Kamala took the remaining three girls into the boom boom room and ate. Meanwhile, the other went into the room with Prince and Tosha and ate Tosha.

"Let me join you," Prince suggested and came behind the groupie. She tilted her ass towards the ceiling as she twirled her tongue around Tosha's lady parts.

Prince eased inside of her and began to stroke. Her tongue darted in and out of Tosha at the same speed and rhythm. Tosha lifted her legs and pulled the girl's face deeper into her crotch by the back of her head. Tosha and Prince came together as they have many times before, whether alone or with company. One time, Tosha, Kamala, Keli and Prince all climaxed at the same time. Proof that there ain't no party like a vampire party, because a vampire party don't stop.

This one did right after the girl bust a creamy nut all over Prince's dick.

Playtime had officially ended and the two vampires bared their fangs and drank every drop of blood from her body.

CHAPTER 9

"Un huh. And just how do you explain this?" Kristine Musa dared as she stood over a man's empty body in the morgue.

"I, umm..." the coroner said and swallowed hard. This time it was he who called her when he examined the man.

He was found in his own vehicle outside of a nightclub the next day. Several dead bodies where reported over the weekend like every weekend in the Atl. This was the only one with bite marks in his neck and not a single drop of body fluid left in his body. Keli sucked his neck so hard, his lungs collapsed, and eyes sunk into his head. There were clear teeth marks right through platinum jewelry he wore.

"That's right, you can't!" she gloated rubbed it in. This was the clearest case of a vampire attack that even she had seen in a while. Most older vampires knew how to conceal their kills to the untrained eye. Some even staged car accidents to cover their consumption. This told her that there was a new vampire in Atlanta. For there to be a new vampire, there had to be an old vampire, since vampires can't just turn themselves. They're not hatched nor do they just fall from the sky.

"I mean, it's um, unusual," he said not quite ready to accept vampires were real. And who could blame him.

"Not unusual for a vampire," she teased as the door came open.

"Sorry, I'm late. I—" Daniel began but got cut off and chewed out.

"No excuse! Miss Musa made it all the way from California and you're right here in the same city!" his boss fussed. His head lowered in shame since he felt guilty about hanging out in the club all night. He stayed at the release party until dawn. He meant to take a five minute power nap but it ended up taking three hours.

"Good afternoon, Daniel," Kristine said and made his raise his head once more.

"Not quite, but good afternoon to you, too," he said and noticed the body on the slab. "I just saw him."

Kristine watched intently as he turned his head and tried to place the face. Of course he looked a lot different now, flushed with death than he did vibrant with life.

"He was found in his truck outside of Club Chaos this morning," the coroner tossed in.

"I was there last night!" Daniel blurted before he could stop himself. It was a good thing he didn't get to get his excuse out since he would have contradicted it. "He was at the release party!"

"Release from prison?" the doctor asked since that's the only thing he knew black men to be released from.

"Album release. A rapper named the Dark Prince! He's a beast!" Daniel said with those same stars in his eyes. Meanwhile, Kristine mulled over his name.

"Dark Prince?" she asked outwardly but inwardly asked herself, *Prince of Darkness?* "Nah."

"What?" Daniel asked of her reaction.

"Nothing," she said and dismissed the silly notion of a rapping vampire. More than likely, some vampire was attracted to all of the people and made a kill. She'd seen this a lot over the years.

"Anyway, I filmed a lot of the show. You can come by later and check it out," he suggested, hoping she would. Kristine cracked a flattered smile at his persistence. She took it as a compliment since guys don't chase ugly chicks.

"Sure," she agreed since ultimately she did want to see that footage. Perhaps should could spot the vampire inside the club.

*****

"Welcome," Daniel greeted as he let Kristine inside his humble abode.

"Quaint. Reminds me of my flat in England," she lied. The man lived in a true bachelor pad with few furnishings. A futon supplied all the seating in the sparse living room. A huge flat screen was mounted on the wall directly across from it. Under it was the latest game consoles and a hundred of the latest games.

"Can I get you something to eat? Drink? I got wings and Coke," he offered hospitably.

"No thanks. I'd rather view this footage you have," she replied.

"Coming right up," he said and grabbed his phone. He synced the phone and TV via Bluetooth and hit play.

"Really dude?" Kristine said and twisted her lips at the porn on the screen.

"My bad," he said even though he meant to do it, hoping the not so subliminal message of girl riding boy backwards might turn her on. He corrected himself and pulled up the video from the show.

"Really, dude?" she repeated and laughed as the video began up Keli's skirt. He fast forwarded past her labia, Tosha's camel toe and Kamala practically naked in the sheer cat suit. Something about the girls stood out to her, but she couldn't put her finger on it. Them moving around while performing didn't allow her to zero in on anything.

"There!" he said and paused the video. He had to back up a few seconds and pointed to the baller who was now in a refrigerated drawer down at the morgue.

"Un huh, that's him," Kristine said as she verified the man on the screen with the pictures she took of his corpse. "Before and after in the worst way!"

"This guy's the truth!" Daniel announced, like a groupie when Prince began to rap offstage.

"God is the truth. Everything else is mediocre," she reminded. That was the truth but when Prince stepped out she felt her pussy twitch. The man was gorgeous and had a magnetism about him that transferred through the video. She, like all of the other women, was stuck until Prince let them go. Her lonely vagina throbbed once more when Prince looked directly at the camera. It was like he was standing. "Can I have a copy of this?"

"Sure! Did you see anything?" he asked as he set up to Bluetooth the video to her.

"No," she said emphatically even though she wasn't sure what she just saw. The only thing she was sure of was the pounding in her panties. "Do you have condoms?"

"Condoms? Yeah, tons of them. Why you—" he asked as the implications caught up with him. "Are you trying to, I mean, you wanna—"

"Can you please stop talking and undress?" she asked and led by example. Her big breasts shut him right up when they debuted in the room. He was stuck in place when the beautiful woman undressed in front of him.

"Oh!" Daniel said when his erection strained to be free and reminded him to undress. He had no idea that Prince just got him some pussy as he led her into his bedroom. The twin mattress was only big enough for either sleeping for one or fucking and that was perfect for Kristine since she didn't plan to spend the night.

"I sure hope you know what you're doing?" Kristine sighed when they settled on his bed. She didn't get much dick since she was too busy hunting vampires.

"Um, yeah!" he said a little more confidently then he felt. He too was pretty busy with work and college. He got lucky here and there but his last "there" was a while ago.

They tried kissing but it was clinical and weird, so they quickly abandoned it. She reached down and gave his dick an inquisitive squeeze, then worked him inside of her. It only took a few strokes for her to realize he wouldn't be able to take her where she was trying to go.

"Okay, stop. Up. On your back," he ordered and took charge. She mounted the man and reached back to put him back inside of her. He had the right size and girth but couldn't work what she needed to be worked. She wiggled and rock until she found her stroke.

"That is better," Daniel had to admit once she got going. He caught on that a rhythm is needed for the stroke to be right. "I think I can—"

"Hush!" she insisted and closed her eyes. She locked eyes with Prince once more, inside her mind and rode. He rode, rocked, and even rolled as an intense orgasm began to slowly build. It started as a tingle in her toes and crept up to her knees. Her thighs tightened and her walls began to contract. Daniel knew what was happening and hoped she would hurry up. A man's orgasm isn't as delicate and deliberate as a woman. It's sudden, impulsive, explosive and was fastly approaching.

"There we go!" she announced with the last three strokes that put her over the edge.

"Argh!" Daniel grunted and sent spurts of wayward babies up into the latex where they could do no harm.

There is a moment right after a mutual climax that hearts make decisions without consulting with the rest of the faculties. Kristine knew that too and rolled off of Daniel and his bed. She wanted no parts of any relationship with anyone so she rushed into his bathroom and under the shower.

"Hole up, I'll join you," Daniel called out from the bed. He basked in the glow of busting a good nut a little too long and she was finished.

"No time for all of that," she declared as she came back out. Joint showers are for couples and she was very much single. The good nut gave her the strength to last until her next moment of weakness.

"I, okay. Well, call me—" he was saying until she rushed from his apartment. The shower could wait so he drifted off to sleep.

CHAPTER 10

"Keli!" Prince roared when he watched the news report of the dead guy at the club. He noticed her slip off and return while he performed and knew she was the culprit.

"Uh oh!" she said when she heard her name boom throughout the house. She knew she was in trouble and hopped up to go face the music. After changing into something to help her case.

"Tell me you didn't drink that man at the club?" he dared before he noticed her nakedness.

"Huh?" she asked and struck a pose. Prince just shook his head and pulled her on the bed. He took out his frustrations between her legs until they were both satisfied.

"Some punishment! I need to be more disobedient myself then," Tosha quipped when she came in just after they both came.

"No, you all must learn to control yourselves! We're going on a national tour and can't leave a trail of bodies everywhere we go," Prince explained.

"Why not? Whose to stop us?" Kamala asked. The other girls turned their heads to hear the answer as well. No one had to tell them that they were atop the food chain. Humans were their food and there was nothing they could do to stop them. As far as they knew that is.

"Because I said so!" he barked just as his mother had decades before in this very room. He was happy to hear the doorbell ring so he could change the subject.

"I'll get it!" Keli sang since she always aimed to please.

"It's Meech, so don't eat him," Prince called after her.

"I wouldn't eat Meech!" she laughed and went to let him in. They were all very fond of Meech for believing in them. She unlocked the door and stepped back to avoid any sunlight that might seep in.

"Hey, Kel. Dayum!" Meech greeted when he saw her in her birthday suit.

"Hey yaself," she giggled and pushed the door closed. "Follow me."

I should have hit that, Meech thought again as her round ass cheeks jiggled in front of him. He was pretty sure Prince was fucking all three of them. He was right too, but had no idea he fucked them all, all day and most of the night. Vampires are insatiable creatures and absolute slaves to their desires.

"Sup, Meech. What's good?" Prince asked. A waste of breath since his guest was stuck on all the ass and ttties in the room.

"I, I umm. Shit, I forgot!" he admitted. The Princesses got a kick out of him and moved provocatively.

"Sales report? Tour?" Prince reminded and got him going again.

"Oh yeah!" he remembered and delivered the news he came with. "You're number one in hip hop downloads and streaming!"

"As I should be," he gloated since being a vampire doesn't prevent hubris.

"They are projected to go number one in R and B when they're released," Meech said and looked between Kamala's open legs. "And the tour starts Friday!"

"We ready!" Prince cheered. He was ready for the world but was the world ready for him!

*****

The tour began in their hometown of Atlanta, then shot up North for shows in New York, New Jersey and Philadelphia. They killed both on and off the stage in each city. Prince packed a supply of plasma but they still selected male and female groupies to feed on after the after party. By the time they reached the Midwest, they left a trail of empties and a pattern. Kristine Musa was an expert on picking up patterns.

"Mmhm!" Kristine hummed in agreement with her nodding head. She was in the Germantown section of Philly looking at a gruesome crime scene.

"Four women were attacked by a pack of wild dogs," the lead detective advised as he showed her the gory crime scene.

"Hyena probably," Kristine offered sarcastically. One such wild dog wandered by and got chased off by a feral cat. "Whew, that was close!"

"Ha ha, vampire lady. I'd believe a pack of hyena over a DM vampire any day!" he shot back. He had been warned the "vampire lady" would he coming when the odd murders were entered into the database.

Kristine knew this was far worse than just a vampire. Worse than even a pack of hyena. This was a pack of vampires, and that was something she'd never seen before. She had heard about packs of vampires and how vicious they could be.

"They're coming back to back," she mumbled to herself as she investigated the crime scene. She had just come from New Jersey and New York and saw the same thing. There was a pattern but she couldn't put her finger on it. Instead, she put her finger on her phone and called her trusty sidekick. Daniel checked in everyday with his findings but also because he was hopelessly in love after their hookup.

"Hey, babe. I—"

"Kristine," she interjected like she had to do any time he used a pet name. She was not babe, boo, sweetie or sugar lumps.

"Okay, Kristine," he relented and sighed. "Anyway, how's Philly? I started to fly up to catch the Dark Prince concert. He's been killing it!"

"Has he?" she asked to let him get it out. Once he finished "fan boy-ing" over the rapper they could get down to business.

"Yes! Packed shows in New York, New Jersey and—"

"Philly? In that order?" she shouted as a pattern came to light.

"Um..." Daniel paused to double check even though he was pretty sure. "Yeah. New York, New Jersey and Philadelphia."

"Where are the next? Tonight!" she demanded.

"Um, next show is in Clev— I mean Cincinnati on Saturday," he decided. Kristine paused at the pause in his reply. There was no reason for the lie that usually accompanies such pauses, so she let it go.

"Okay. Keep your ears and eyes open. I'll call you from Cincinnati!" she blurted as goodbye and clicked off.

"No, I'll see you in Cincinnati," he corrected. "But first, I have a little stop in Cleveland!"

*****

"I'm hungry!" Keli pouted as the tour bus rolled into Cleveland Ohio.

"Well run out and grab someone to eat!" Tosha fussed. It was broad daylight outside of the blacked out bus so she knew she wasn't going anywhere.

Prince maintained his discipline but the girls had none. Even he knew it was becoming a problem by the time they reached Ohio. He could only hope to hold on because they stood to make millions more on the tour. If they could could finish, that is.

"Look!" Kamala cheered excitedly and thrust her phone under Prince's nose. Their debut album had shot to the top of the R and B charts just as expected.

"As it should be! We rule the world," Prince nodded arrogantly. Jay-A said it best that "Fame is the worst drug known to man" and Prince was feeling himself.

"We do, daddy," Tosha purred and slid up next to him.

"Cut it out. All of you!" Prince ordered as he heard the malicious thoughts bouncing around in their heads. All three had been inseparable since Dora the explorer lunch boxes and panties. Now they all had thoughts of killing each other and going solo.

Keli stormed off and grabbed a couple of plasma packs from the fridge and curbed her thirst. They all rested up for the show later that night in the house that Lebron built. Once nightfall fell, they exited the bus and breathed in the night air.

"After the show," Prince told Keli and put a fanged smile on her face.

"After the show," she agreed even though the burly stagehands were looking scrumptious. She licked her lips at a four hundred pound security guard and made him blush.

"After the show," Kamala seconded as she eyed a snack of her own. Prince knew his control over the girls was less than their desires. He just hoped they could keep it together until the end of the tour.

Meanwhile, an amateur vampire hunter had landed in town and rushed over to the stadium.

*****

"Medical," Daniel said in an authoritarian tone when he reached the entrance for the dressing room and backstage. He flashed his credentials from work and breezed by the guard.

"Okay," the man said and stepped aside. He was on guard for female groupies and let the male groupie slide right by.

Daniel couldn't decide if he was a groupie or vampire hunter as he toured the backstage area of the nations hottest tours. B-list rappers floated around like the weed smoke hovering in the air. He stopped and bobbed his head as they rapped in circles to prepare for their opening acts.

Meanwhile, the main act warmed up inside the hot vaginas of his Princesses. The insatiable foursome had a foursome that would only curb their appetites just like the packs of plasma. After the show, the after party would be an orgy of blood and sex and violence for whatever unlucky groupie selected.

"Here we go," Daniel said as he reached the dressing room with the girls name on it. Unlike Kristine, he didn't think Prince could be a vampire and hoped to disprove it before they reached Cincinnati. Then he would be able to get a second helping of her insides.

"Medical!" he announced and turned the knob. The door opened and he eased inside the empty room. He began a search of the room, looking for evidence that proved they were human. Instead, he found a pair of frilly panties that caught his attention. Most men will sniff for a whiff of pussy and he was no exception.

"You like?" a voice asked behind him while he had the crotch in his nostrils, inhaling the sweet remnants of a clean vagina.

"It's not what it looks like!" he said and snatched them away from his face and spun around to face the face belonging to the voice.

"It looked like you were smelling my panties?" Keli asked and cracked her pretty smile.

"Huh? Oh, no. I was just, umm... Medical," he said and held up his badge once again.

"This isn't Atlanta," she reminded since she was able to read the badge in the brief second he displayed it. She smiled again, lifted a leg, and slid a finger inside of herself. "Here..."

Keli didn't yet posses powers of hypnosis but he came none the less. He inhaled the wet finger before letting her slide it in his mouth. Daniel had no idea some of the juice he sucked from her finger belonged to Prince.

"Why are you here?" Keli asked. She had always been a smart girl and knew a medical examiner from Atlanta in her dressing room in Cincinnati was no coincidence.

"My um, friend. Well, she thinks... It's crazy but, are you a vampire?" he stammered.

"Yes," she answered and bared her fangs. "And now you are, too!"

Daniel couldn't even scream when Keli clamped on his neck. She reached inside his pants and massaged his meat while draining his blood. She almost went too far but let up when his knees buckled under him.

She lowered him to the ground and slit her nipple with her claw. She put him on her titty like a baby and let him drink. The flow of blood flowed into his mouth and brought him back from the brink of death. He would still die anyway but would then be reborn.

Keli stuffed Daniel into a closet and went to perform. He was lucky to catch the before party because no one would survive the after party.

CHAPTER 11

"Thank you, Cleveland!" Prince declared when he brought his show to a close. He had performed his entire album and a plethora of unreleased material. Video of the performance was viral before he stepped off the stage.

"Cincinnati, huh?" Kristine fussed when the video hit the Gram. She knew Daniel didn't just omit a whole city by mistake. She called his phone repeatedly but only got to leave messages since he was currently going from life to death and back to life.

A hundred faithful followers followed the flock over to the nightclub hosting the after party. The after party "party" would be held in a five star hotel. One selected for the incinerator they used to dispose of their garbage.

"Thanks for coming!" the owner of the club greeted as he let Prince and the Princesses into the back door. The club was packed and a line of people who were not getting in stretched around the block.

"Thank me for coming," Prince insisted. He was promised ten thousand extra dollars to grace his place with face. Tosha stuck her hand out to collect the fee.

"I'm umm, am a little short," he stammered and parted with three of the promised ten thousand dollars.

"You mean a lot short!" Kamala growled and nearly showed her fangs. The club was at capacity and charging twenty bucks a head. The busy bartenders were proof that the greedy man was trying to get over on them.

"Can I?" Keli dared.

"You sure can. Just not here," Prince said and turned to the only. "That's fine. Come back to the hotel afterwards. I think she likes you."

"I do like him!" Keli purred and gripped his crotch. She felt him grow stiff in her hand and said, "I see he likes me, too!"

"We do!" he said on behalf of him and his dick. He rushed off to call home and make some excuses to his wife. He planned to cheat on her just like he just cheated his guest out of most of their fee. It would have been a stellar night if not for a date with death.

Prince held court in the VIP section, taking pictures with hood celebrities and thots. He had selected two women for himself and let the girls pick out a few for themselves. He felt the presence of another vampire and went on high alert.

"Bonjour," Butta greeted as a sarcastic reminder of their mutual place of rebirth. Prince braced himself against the shiver that always ran up his spine whenever he thought of Katrina. He had been deathly afraid of the woman but hearing Butta had dispatched her gave him reason to now fear him. He did, but it didn't show.

"Bonjour, monsieur," Prince said and pushed the groupie by his side away so Butta could sit. She had been in the midst of jacking his dick, so he left it out as a show of disrespect.

"I'll stand," he said and let his fangs hang to show what he thought of being chumped off. Little did Prince know, he followed the tour and left bodies behind in his wake. It was as if he was marking a trail. "I enjoyed the show."

"I enjoyed yours in Atlanta. Kinda reckless leaving headless bodies in the park?" Prince said with a question mark to get an answer.

"Eh," and a nonchalant shrug was all he had coming.

"Coming to the after party?" he asked.

"So you and your little entourage can attack? We shall dance our dance, just not tonight," he laughed. He mentally demanded the groupie to stand and she did. She took two steps towards Butta until Prince butted into her brain.

She spun around and took three steps in his direction. Butta commanded her to turn around again and she did. The two vampires played a game of tug a war within her brain that caused her nose to bleed. They reached a draw when she passed out from the pressure.

"Let's go," Prince directed when the commotion around the girl began. He quickly replaced her with another and led the way out of the club.

"I'll ride with you," Keli told the club owner when they stepped outside.

"As long as you ride this dick," he bargained.

"But of course I'll ride this horse! Like you never been rode before!" she said and gripped it once again. Once again, it grew hard in her hand and sealed his fate.

Prince had rented half a floor for his nighttime festivities. There was only an hour before the sun obeyed its Lord and rose from the east. Blackout curtains would give them a few more hours of playtime.

"It's playtime!" Keli announced when they reached a room. She quickly stripped but found the man had still beat her getting undressed. By the time she looked up, he was wearing was his socks and a smile. His erection stood straight out ahead, bobbing in mid air.

"Tah dah!" he playfully pronounced to present his penis.

"Well, I can't ride it like that," Keli lied. She rode Prince while he stood just this morning but preferred to have the man on his back.

He dove on his back on the bed and pointed his dick to the sky. Keli rushed over and did an acrobatic flip onto the dick like it was the Olympics. He should have known something was wrong then but couldn't ignore the sexy young thing riding his dick. Even when she moved at superhuman speed.

"Okay then, lil' bit!" he cheered when she spun around and rode him backwards, and sideways. The next time she spun, she bore her fangs and rode even faster. This would have been a good time to panic, but he just cheered her on. "Get it, lil' mama!"

Keli bust a good nut then bit into his neck. A satisfying gush of hot blood filled her mouth when she latched on. The man fought and struggled to no avail. He ended up being food for a hungry vampire.

The same was going on down the hall in the presidential suite. Prince and the remaining Princesses had a blood soaked orgy with several more groupies. Once their lust was satisfied, Prince collected the corpses and escorted them to the incinerator. Their work was done in Cleveland and it was time to move on to Cincinnati.

*****

"Hey! What are you doing here?" a janitor fussed when he found a man stuffed in the closet. He was startled at first, thinking he had come across a corpse. The dead body moved when he poked it with his broom so he knew he was alive.

"I. I umm..." Daniel started and stopped because he didn't know what or where he was. He extricated himself from the closet and stood.

"I'm calling the cops," he decided and turned to do just that.

"Wait!" Daniel said and grabbed his arm in a panic. Both were shocked when he easily flung him across the room.

"What the fuck?" Daniel asked aloud as the events leading to him being found in the closet came back to him. "No!"

"Okay, I won't call the cops! Just leave. I have to get this dressing room ready for the concert," he pleaded.

"The Dark Prince concert?" he asked and held his breath for the answer that would confirm or deny his suspicions.

"Dark Prince? That was two days ago! Have you been here all that time? You were sleep for two days!" the janitor reeled. He just knew it had to be some of these new fangled drugs the kids used nowadays. Back in his day, they had to smoke it, or shoot it, maybe even snort it up their nostrils. Now they have stuff you just lick and it'll keep you high for a week.

"Sleep? Nah, I was dead," Daniel said and accepted his fate.

"Dead?" the man asked and began to ease backwards towards the door.

"Yeah, now I'm undead. A vampire," he explained and the man made a run for it.

Daniel made a leap across the room and landed on his back before he could get the door open. He reached turned his head around the wrong way with a sickening crunch of bone and cartilage. That first bite into human flesh is just like that first hit of any drug. A satisfying feeling flowed through Daniel's body as he drank the life nectar of another. He could feel life flowing into him and it felt good.

Keli didn't just create a vampire, she created a monster.

*****

Kristine still hadn't heard from Daniel and was beginning to worry. The man would call or text her daily, but now she hadn't heard from him in days. She ignored the carnage left in Cleveland and landed in Cincinnati.

Butta had left a deliberate mess behind in every city the tour made a stop. His was the pattern she was following since the missing persons hadn't reached her radar.

The mutilated body found in a five star hotel put Kristine in the right direction. She called around and found out which one was booked tight for the night of the concert and headed right over.

"I need a suite," she insisted when she reached the counter.

"We're completely booked," the pretty lady behind the counter countered.

"Interpol," she said and produced her credentials. Completely booked has a different meaning with the right badge. Most hotels hold a couple rooms for last minute VIPs and the international police fit the criteria.

"Room 12-26. I hope it's not too loud up there. A concert is in town and the entourage is staying on the twelfth floor, as well," she apologized in advance.

"Loud is good," Kristine replied. She knew how loud a vampire would scream when the sunrays set them on fire. Her bag was packed with the tools of her trade including stakes, and garlic. She also had pure silver in various forms including bullets for a silencer-equipped pistol she packed. Still she hoped to try her vaccine on a living specimen so she could rid the world of vampires once and for all.

Kristine may have spent her life hunting immortals but she was very much mortal herself. She let out a queen sized yawn as soon she saw the king size bed in her room. There was plenty of time before the show for her to nap so she climbed on and drifted away.

*****

"I'm hungry!" Keli sung her usual song. She knew what was coming and pulled a pack of plasma from the fridge.

"What are we going to do about Butta? He's a problem!" Tosha declared and bared her fangs to show her solution.

"He's more than just a problem..." Prince said and trailed off. Once again, he thought about how powerful Butta must be to have killed Katrina. A vampire can only gain strength from killing other vampires. He knew what had to be done once they returned to Atlanta. They had to turn and kill as many new vampires as possible before Butta made his move.

He wasn't the only one planning to turn and kill other vampires. The girls were smart enough not to think it when in his presence but all had the same idea. The same idea, yet for different reasons.

Tosha wanted to be the queen to King Prince and could do without the other Princesses. Keli wanted to be stronger so she could feed when and how she wanted. She had a head start on her friends since she had Daniel's address from his work credentials. Kamala smelled smoke from her friends and knew she had to protect herself. There could be only one and she planned to be it.

"Well, it's showtime," Prince announced once the sun had finally set. Now they could venture out and select their prey for the after party. They lined up their meals and headed over to the stadium to put on their show.

*****

"Shit!" Kristine fussed when she willed herself awake. She had slept through the alarm she set for herself. She popped up and rushed under the shower to wake herself up completely. Vampire hunting is no place for the drowsy.

She still had to be cute, so she dressed to impress. A squirt of garlic perfume on her neck would at least slow a vampire down. The silver bullets in her small automatic would drop him dead on the spot if hit in the heart. It was easier to conceal than the crossbow with the wooden stakes that worked just as well. She finished dressing and rushed from her room and came face to face with a vampire.

"Well, hello there," Butta greeted with the unmistakable charisma of a vampire. Kristine froze for a split second from the shock, then regained her composure.

"Hello, yourself," she purred and cleared her mind of any thoughts. Butta frowned when her mind went blank, leaving him nothing to read. She couldn't read his mind either and he had plans to leave a surprise for Prince when he returned.

"Care to spend a little time with me?" he invited and extended an elbow to escort her.

"Sure," she said, accepting the invitation and elbow. He escorted her straight to Prince's room and used the key the housekeeper gave him. The Mexican woman was in his tub right now waiting to be devoured for dinner. He would plant her empty corpse so the heat would fall on Prince when the bodies began to all connect back to him.

"Nice," she sang as they entered the room.

"Nice indeed," Butta said as he checked out her ass. She put a little extra on it as a distraction and distracted him enough to pull her weapon.

"Sorry," she said in advance and whirled around with the syringe.

"You will be!" Butta growled as he caught the needle in his hand. She managed to inject half of the solution before he could snatch it out. A viscous backhand lifted her off her feet and deposited her across the room. Her head hit the wall hard enough to nearly crack her skull. She was sound asleep as she slid down to the carpet below.

Butta took one step in her direction until he began to feel the effects of what she shot him up with. First, the sedation of the silver in the solution. It was enough to drop him to one knee like Colin Kapernick. He tried to stand once more but wobbled and fell.

Prince would easily take his head off if found him in this condition. All he could do was crawl out of the room and down the hall. He hit the stairwell and fell down one flight to his own floor. Butta barely made it to his own room and into the bathroom. He found the housekeeper curled up into a fetal ball where he left her. His fangs wouldn't extend, so he gnawed his way into her wrist and saved his life.

******

Hours later, Prince and company arrived back to his room. Four women and two men were selected for the festivities of fucking and feasting. Prince stopped dead in his tracks the moment he opened the door.

"Wait!" he demanded from the remnants of Butta left in the air. The faint heartbeat drew his eyes to Kristine unconscious on the floor. "Go to your room."

"But we—" Kamala began to protest but got shutdown before she could get it out.

"Go!" Prince boomed and they were gone. Keli smiled since it was more for her. He turned his head curiously and approached the woman on the floor. Checking her pulse proved his ears correct and he knew she was close to death.

"Sho' nuff," Prince chuckled as he read the thoughts bouncing around beneath her skull. She could control her thoughts when she was awake but had no protection from his probing while unconscious. Plus, she was fine as Prince noticed when he looked her over.

Prince saw her memories of the mother she lost to a vampire and her subsequent vendetta against his kind. She was here to destroy him, so he wasn't sure why he picked her up and headed over to the window. It was quicker to jump than wait for an elevator, so he made the leap. Prince landed twelve flights down as smoothly as a cat and took off towards the hospital. He blended with the wind and was there moments later.

"Take this empty gurney over to—" a doctor was saying until the ER door flew open. He and the orderly saw the black blur but neither could comprehend what just happened. "Anyway, take this—"

He stopped in his tracks once more when he noticed the body of a woman on the once empty gurney. The two men looked to each other for explanation but neither had one. They did have a woman near death and quickly moved to move her back to life.

Meanwhile, Prince returned and rummaged through her bag. He took notice of the weapons of his destruction. It led him back to her room where he found even more information on her mission. Dawn had crept up while he read her notes in her laptop. They explained the strange fluid in the syringe.

"This might help you out," Prince said and made a few adjustments to her formula. He took an empty syringe and filled it with the one component she was missing. Blood from a vampire.

The rest of the tour went off without a hitch with Butta and Kristine out of the picture. One was permanently disfigured and the other was fighting for her life. Both fully recovered but would be forever changed.

CHAPTER 12

"Uh oh!" one Hollywood hooker shouted when a luxury vehicle pulled onto the hoe stroll on Hollywood boulevard. She took two steps towards the Benz when a younger hooker kicked her foot and tripped her on her face. The nimble nympho hopped the downed prostitute like a hurdle at a track meet, and ran over to the car. Selling pussy is a contact sport on any hoe stroll.

"Date, mister?" she asked as she hopped her happy ass on his passenger seat. She was already in when she saw how hideous he was.

Only one of Butta's fangs would extend and his claws were out permanently. The effects of the silver hung around like a case of herpes. His days of seducing his dinner was over. He was now just a monster who hunted at night for prey. His only solution was also to turn and kill other vampires so he could regain his strength.

"I would love a date," he slurred and slobbered. He also produced the stack of hundreds that kept her from jumping right back out of the car. She had done a lot more for a whole lot less money than he extended.

The woman clutched the money and dipped into his lap as he drove. She worked her neck while he whipped in and out of traffic. The dead dick didn't even get hard but she kept on working hard. Butta drove with a purpose until he reached their spot. His next stop of the night and her last stop in this life.

"We're here," Butta announced and pulled his flaccid dick away as he got out.

"Un uh! I don't do no homes!" she protested when she realized he pulled up to his house. It was a good rule to have since women where going missing from the track every night.

Butta kept on walking and walked into his home. She could either follow him inside or take her chances with the pumas of the

Hollywood hills. She decided to go into the million-dollar home instead of tangling with mountain lions.

"Hello? Mister!" she called out as she gingerly entered the mansion. Her apprehension lifted as she looked around the swanky home.

I'm gone fuck his ugly ass to death, she decided and went further inside.

"Sit," Butta directed when she reached his den. She still didn't see him but complied. He went to check on his crop while she awaited.

"Where am I?" the prostitute asked when she awoke as Butta walked into a room. She had been slinging ass on Hollywood Boulevard when she got picked up. He had several fermenting in his home every day.

"Hell!" Butta declared and attacked. She was too weak from just being dead to put up much of a fight. He clamped his mouth over her neck and let his lone fang sink into her jugular vein.

Butta felt the surge of life as he drank the blood of the new vampire. Her virgin fangs and claws extended but she would never get to use them. Butta sucked her dry and beyond and then twisted her head completely around. He stood and looked down as his dick began to harden and stretch.

"Ah yes!" he cheered as his other fang extended. He willed them up and down and they worked once again. Now it was time to put his resurgent erection back to work.

"Hey! Y'all gonna have to pay extra if there's two of you!" the woman protested when Butta walked back in on her looking like a new man. She hoped her fuss made him forget seeing her collecting trinkets from around the room and putting them in her purse and pockets.

"But of course!" he smiled and approached. She clutched the extra money he handed over before shoving himself inside of her. He lifted her by one ankle and slung the dick like a Frisbee.

Butta was generous enough to get her rocks of before biting her neck. He was already full from the vampire he just finished and only needed a sip. That's all that is needed to turn a mortal into an immortal. Using his fangs, he opened his own wrist and forced her to drink. He tossed her in the room with two others in various states of vampire fermentation. Once she was ripe, he would add her to a growing list as he bounded back from Kristine's so-called cure.

*****

Kristine woke up two days later in the same hospital Prince dropped her off. She laid there with her eyes closed and just listened for a few hours to get her bearings. She gleamed her medical condition was improved and she could he discharged soon.

"Well, hello there, young lady!" the doctor cheered when she blinked awake. The nurse rushed over to check her vitals and her bedpan.

"How are you feeling?" the woman asked as she updated her chart. According to her vital signs, she was just fine but wanted to hear it from her.

"Fine," Kristine replied despite the splitting headache. "Can I go?"

"Not so fast. You have a hairline fracture. A concussion—" the doctor warned. It was all precautionary but the answer was, no.

"How did my stuff get here?" she cut in and asked when she saw her phone and laptop bag on the bedside table.

"Your boyfriend bought them last night!" the nurse blushed and gushed.

"My who?" she asked and thought of Daniel. He must have come to town and found her. She leaned up and looked around to see if he was still here.

"Who, she says!" the woman gushed some more. "Dating the hottest rapper on the planet and she says, who?"

Kristine looked towards the doctor for help but he just shrugged. He preferred Punjabi music to hip hop, so it didn't register with him. Luckily for the woman, she had secured a selfie and pulled it up on her phone. The nurse was all smiles while Kristine frowned in confusion.

"He brought my laptop?" she asked as she looked at the smiling nurse hugged up with the Dark Prince. He peered directly into her soul even through the photograph.

"And your car keys. Said everything is in there," the woman relayed. What she didn't relay was the sloppy blow job she gave him in the bathroom.

"Hmph," Kristine wondered since the "everything" she brought along was everything she needed to kill vampires. "Can I have my laptop?"

"Sure. Just rest up and you may be able to go home in a day or two," the doctor answered when the nurse deferred the question to him.

Kristine turned her computer so no one could see the encrypted login she used. It only got her as far as the iris scan that led her to the fingerprint scan. Once the biometric security was satisfied, she entered the nickname her father gave her so she would be allowed entry.

"Choo-choo" she typed and smiled at the distant memories she had of the man.

"What the—" she gasped, causing a reaction in the machines she was still hooked up to. They beeped and whirled in concert with her shock as she slammed the laptop closed again.

"What's wrong!" the nurse asked in near panic as he vitals went haywire.

"Nothing. Excuse me," Kristine said as she instantly regained her cool. The nurse frowned at the equipment and blamed it for the glitch. No one can go from zero to a hundred and back to zero in five seconds.

"Buzz if you need help with anything," the woman offered as she left the room.

"Sure," she lied since the nurse certainly couldn't help her with her problems. She eased the laptop open again and came face to face with a vampire. Kristine lifted her chin to show she wasn't afraid and pressed play on the frozen video on the screen.

"As salaamu alaykum, Miss Musa. You are a very interesting lady. I am quite impressed!" Prince began. He paused to let her process him being in her computer, then continued.

"I know why you are doing what you're doing. I am sorry about your mother, but I don't want you to end up like her. I feed on the disposables, unessentials, superfluous, superficial people."

"No such thing!" she fussed at the screen.

"I knew you would say that!" he laughed and made her check to see if they were live. They were not and he went on. "Notice the world hasn't paused for any of them. Not a one. Now, I looked over your formula and made a few changes. I don't know if you're on to something or not, but I did fix a few obvious errors in your design."

"I didn't make any errors! It's just a matter of dosage. Once I figure that out—"

"I knew you would say that, too!" he laughed. A deep resonating laugh that vibrated her lady parts. Kristine blushed at her own reaction and continued to listen. "I left you a present. To help you help me. Now, for a little entertainment..."

Kristine felt helpless against the hypnotic pull when he ordered her to put her hand between her legs. She spread her thighs as commanded and began to massage her vagina. It soon soaked her fingers when she parted her labia and found her swollen clit.

"Ssss!" Kristine hissed. She followed directions and turned on the video chat to a live feed of Prince. He had a pair of her panties in his hand as Kamala bobbed and gagged as she pleasured him while watching her pleasure herself.

"Will you cum for me?" Prince asked in that deep baritone voice of his. He turned off his hypnosis so she could stop if she wanted to.

"Yesss. Mmhm, yes!" she moaned and pressed on. The squishing of her sopping wet pussy echoed in the otherwise quiet room. Soon her soft whimpers sang backup to her vagina.

"Can I see?" he asked, using just his charm. It was enough for her to tilt the screen to show her vagina. He was thoroughly impressed with her pretty, plump, pinkness.

"See? Mmm!" Kristine moaned again. Her legs bucked as an intense orgasm shook her soul. Prince grunted and filled Kamala's mouth as quickly as she could swallow.

"That was our first time cumming together. It will not be our last," Prince said. He ended with a stern warning, "Don't end up like your mother."

"Shit!" Kristine fussed when he clicked away from the live feed. She snatched her hand out of her wet snatch and dried her fingers on the sheet. Her next stop was her formulas to see what he had changed. The scowl on her face began to relax once she read what he wrote. "This just might work? Now all I need is a vampire!"

Kristine was discharged the next day and found her car parked in the lot. She was shocked to see everything was still there. Besides the panties, he took as a trophy all her devices to kill his kind were in tact. She also found two vials of blood. Vampire blood.

CHAPTER 13

Daniel wasn't used to being such a chick magnet but that's exactly what he had become since becoming a vampire. He found out the perils of daylight the hard way in the week since he awoke. Now he too prowled the night in search of prey. The easiest prey was found in the nightclubs of Atlanta. He stalked them like a beast of prey does a watering hole in the wild.

"Hey!" a perky white girl sang and bounced as he stepped into the club. He chose this particular club tonight since it had a reputation for multinationals partying together in harmony.

He was in a ghetto club the night before and drank his fill once a shootout in the parking lot left several patrons leaking on the pavement. That only filled one lust, so tonight he sought to fill another.

"Hey ya'self, beautiful!" he said with his newfound charm. He extended an elbow to escort her to the bar for a drink. Several actually since alcohol thins out the blood and allows it to flow smoothly. Not that Daniel was a smooth vampire. He was not. In fact, he was becoming quite the savage.

They posted up at the bar and exchanged names. They went from total strangers to Daniel and Mandy. A few drinks later, they were kissing on the bar stool while he played in her pussy under the short skirt she wore. She came to get laid, so she didn't bother wearing any panties.

"Let's get out of here," he suggested. Come to find out, playing in the pussy is just as effective as hypnosis.

"Let's before I cum all over your fingers! Only you have to eat my pussy!" she demanded. Many of her one-night stands ended up one sided. She wanted to make sure she got off, too, so she made sure to get off first.

"Oh, I definitely plan to eat the pussy!" he said with a sinister laugh as he led her from the club.

Mandy was a generous thot and leaned over to blow him while he drove. Daniel circled his block twice until he skeeted on her tonsils. He rushed her upstairs and into his bedroom. He kept his word and dipped below her waist. He twirled his tongue around her tight twat like a blender. She quickly returned the favor and came in his mouth. Daniel rushed up her body and plunged inside of her.

"Wait, you have to put on a rubber!" she protested in rhythm with his rough stroke.

"Don't worry. You can't catch what I have," he assured her. She kept on protesting and he kept on stroking. All was forgotten when she bust a nut on his bare dick. He snatched out at the last second and bust on her stomach.

"Thank you," she sighed as she leaned up and watched him paint her stomach with come.

"I still wanna eat your pussy," he explained. His fangs slowly came down as he kissed between her legs. He planted a loud kiss on her to wet labia before biting the entire mound of flesh completely away.

Mandy let out such a high-pitched scream only dogs could hear it. Scooby Doo was nowhere in sight and her ass was in trouble. He gulped down her lips and leaned into the resulting gush of blood. The woman slipped into a state of shock as she was drained completely dry by the vampire.

"Refreshing!" Daniel said after he finished his meal. He showered the sex and violence away and got dressed once more. After checking to make sure the coast was clear, he slipped Mandy's empty shell out to his car. He drove her over to the hood and dumped her in a dumpster. She would be found just like the others and they were beginning to add up.

*****

"You guys killed it!" Meechie cheered when Prince and the girls returned to Atlanta. As frugal as he and Angela were, they were set for life. Even before royalties and other income began pouring in.

"You can say that again!" Keli snickered. She managed to make and murder two vampires while away on the road. One was a security guard, the other a male groupie who followed the group. More importantly, she managed to keep Prince out of her head.

"Good to be home," Prince sighed. Vampire or no vampire, being on tour is a lot of work. He couldn't wait to sleep in his own bed and hunt in his own city.

"Well rest up, cuz we got fifty dates set up overseas!" Meech cheered with dollar signs in his eyes. Not for himself, but to keep his word to make his client rich and famous.

"Cool," Prince nodded as he went inside Meechie's mind. All he saw was good inside of the man. Especially with the malicious thoughts Tosha had while looking at Kamala. Kamala smiled and wished death upon her, as well. He was used to that, but it was Keli who made him frown. He got nothing when he peeked inside her frontal lobe where the immediate thoughts are kept. He wasn't a betting vampire but if he was, his money would be on her.

"Well, I'll see you guys tomorrow at the station," their manager said and stood.

"What happens tomorrow? At the station?" Prince asked since it was the first he heard of it.

"They wanna interview you on the morning show!" he gushed like the big deal it was.

"I don't do mornings. Not yet—" Prince said and thought about his long term goals. He would one day be a day walker and walk around freely by day or night.

"Yeah, I forgot y'all be partying all night and sleeping all day! I'll see how we can get it done!" Meech said like the good manager he was becoming. His phone, inbox, DM and email were all full of prospective clients wanting him to make them a star.

"I'll walk him out," Keli suggested once the meeting wrapped up.

"We want to see him again," Prince reminded. Everyone laughed except Meech since he wasn't a vampire and didn't get the vampire humor. He laughed anyway just to fit in and let Keli walked him out.

Dang I wanna fuck you!' Meech thought beneath his smile as they headed to the door.

"You can, you know?" Keli replied out loud when she realized she could now hear thoughts.

"Can what?" Meech frowned fearful that he had thought aloud.

"Fuck me. You just said you wanna fuck me. You can. Let's hook up sometime. Just don't let Prince and the other girls know," she offered.

"O—okay," he stammered unsurely. Every man will eventually be tested in their life and relationships. She pressed her fine frame against his chubby one and stuffed her tongue down his throat. Meech felt his knees buckle from getting so hard so quickly. It was all he could do to pull away and rush out of the house. He sped home to fuck his girl and saved his life.

*****

"Answer your phone!" Kristine fussed as Daniel's phone just rang. It ended up at his voicemail but she still refused to leave a message. Instead, she sped over to the morgue to chew him out in person.

She hadn't heard a word from him since he lied about the tours next stop. Now she had several possible vampire attacks in his own city and he hadn't reached out to her. Deep in her heart, she expected the worse. If he ran into Prince in Cleveland, he was already dead or worse.

"M—mi, mi, Musa," the medical examiner stuttered when she walked in the morgue.

"No vampire lady?" she questioned curiously and cocked her head. Something clearly had him shook and she wanted to know what.

"We, ha—have t—two un—unexplained murders. They don't make any sense!" he said.

"Where is Daniel?" Kristine asked when a scan of the room didn't produce him or the other death doctor.

"Good question. He took off one day and never came b—back. Doctor Andrews quit when we got this last one," he said and pointed at the corpse on a slab. He pointed from across the room as if he didn't want to go near it. Kristine did and quickly crossed the room. She approached from the head and didn't see any obvious signs of trauma. A lot of vampire attacks end in a broken neck just from the force of feeding. The woman on the slab neck was straight and no signs of bite marks.

"I don't see an—" Kristine was saying as she moved towards her midsection. The sight of her ravaged crotch stopped her in her tracks.

"I've n—never seen anyth—thing like that before in my life!" the doctor said, keeping his distance.

"I have," she said as her own mother's crime scene photos came to mind. Her mother had been mauled but not quite as savagely as this. This was the work of an animal. "The other?"

"Drawer six, six—sixteen," the doctor said, still stuttering. Kristine walked over and pulled out the drawer. It was another clear case of vampire overkill. Signs of a new vampire, finding himself.

"Vampires are real," Kristine insisted. The doctor nodded but that wasn't good enough. "No. Say it!"

"I mean, I certainly can't explain how this is highly irregular—"

"Say it!" Kristine Musa barked loud enough to wake the dead if such a thing were possible. It isn't so they slept right through it.

"Vampires are real!" he said with the awe that comes with realization of supernatural events. Science couldn't explain what was laying on the table but Kristine could.

"Vampires are very real and they're here. In Atlanta!" she assured him.

*****

Kristine called Daniel's phone all the way from his job to his doorstep. The answer was the same no answer she had been getting since she woke up in the hospital. She parked and hopped out her car to go inside. A last second thought made her put a few etceteras in her purse. His car was in it's parking spot, so she marched inside.

"Daniel! Open this door!" Kristine demanded and pounded. She recognized the muted music playing on the other side of the door since she had been studying everything she could on the Dark Prince. Except his videos since she felt guilty about playing in her pussy at his suggestion.

"Go away!" Daniel shouted when he realized she wasn't going away.

"Have it your way!" she yelled back. Daniel thought he had run her off until she kicked the door.

"Stop it!" he shouted. He knew first hand how strong her legs were and that the flimsy apartment door wouldn't take too many more kicks.

"Then let me in!" she demanded, punctuating each word with another kick.

"I told you to go away!" Daniel growled as he snatched his door open. He bared his fangs in hopes of scaring her off.

"Oh, Daniel!" Kristine moaned when one of her fears were confirmed. She had hoped he was killed instead of turned into a vampire. "No! What did you do?"

"I was reborn! I feel like a new man!" he said as she barged inside. Her eyes immediately shot over to the corpse in the corner.

"No, you're a monster!" she fussed. She took a step to check on the woman until she saw the greenish tint of death in her face. "I can help you."

"You mean your so-called cure that kills? No thanks," he declined.

"You have to let me help you. You can't just kill people," she pleaded.

"People are my food. You should join me. Prince has his Princesses. You can be my queen!" he decided.

"Did he do this to you?" Kristine demanded hotly.

"No. Keli did," he replied. "I never got to the Dark Prince."

"And she is going to come back and kill you! You know they turn vampires to kill so they can gain strength!" the expert reminded. Come to find out she was preaching to the choir when the corpse in the corner began to fidget.

"Almost ripe," Daniel cheered happily. He did know that and was trying to gain strength, as well.

Kristine reached into her bag and came out with one of the many items inside. She rushed across the room and stabbed the dead women in her heart with small wooden stake.

"Stay dead," she told the woman and turned to Daniel.

"What did you do that for? Is that what you plan to do to me?" he asked as his fangs and claws began to slowly slide out.

"No. I'm going to fix you. This can cure you," she said and pulled a syringe from her bag. She had tweaked her formula using Prince's help. It removed the virus from his blood in a lab test. Now it was time for a human trial on an inhuman.

"I don't want to be cured!" he snapped and crossed the room in a blur. He slapped the syringe away and caused it to lodge in the ceiling. "I'm going to cure you!"

"Nah, I'm good," Kristine said and pulled her other hand from behind her back. She quickly fired a round in each leg that dropped him to his knees.

"Wanna see a cool trick?" the vampire laughed and began to push the bullets back out of his body. He had spent the last week harming himself so he could heal himself. A frown furrowed his brow when it wouldn't work.

"Yeah, no it doesn't work with silver bullets," she explained and put a round in each arm. The silver made him weak enough for her to approach. She used a dining room chair to retrieve the syringe from the ceiling.

"Don't! It'll kill me. I'm too young to die!" Daniel pleaded. Kristine replied by looking over at the young dead girl in the corner.

"Bismillah," Kristine said and inserted the needle into his jugular in the name of God. She stood, took two steps back, and pulled her phone.

"I—I feel, it," Daniel said as the solution flowed through his system. He growled and fought against the cure with all his might while she recorded him.

Kristine's mind ran through the formula once again as he churned and twisted defiantly. She wondered what she missed. Why wasn't it working? Then, it started to work.

Daniel let out a tremendous roar as his fangs began to retract. Next, his long claws slid back up into his fingers. He was still fighting the whole way as he returned to normal, returned to mortal.

"Welcome back," Kristine smiled as his breathing became regular.

"I told you not to!" he moaned when he realized it had worked. He opened his mouth to say more but suddenly grabbed his chest like Fred Sanford. His face screwed up to match the pressure in his chest.

"What? No! Um..." Kristine said in a panic. She knew a heart attack when she saw one but calling 911 wasn't exactly an option. She had no choice other than watch the man die.

Not before refilling the syringe with his blood, so she could figure out what she missed. The cure should have worked but instead, it killed instead.

CHAPTER 14

"I'm going out. I ordered dinner, so you girls behave," Prince ordered once the sun set.

"Okaaaaay," the girls sang just like the R and B group they were. They had been singing together since they were five years old and sang as one.

"Hmph," he said and twisted his lips. The malicious thoughts floating around the room almost made him abandon his mission.

Prince hated to leave them alone but South Carolina beckoned. He sensed a vampire at his show there a few weeks ago. He only got a glimpse of the young white woman while he performed but she was gone by the time he finished his set. Now that his schedule allowed, he planned to pay her a little visit.

Ultimately he decided to leave, so he ordered them a big meal that should keep them busy for a while. Anderson was only a two hour drive but much shorter on foot. If you're a vampire, that is.

"Be good," he advised once more and took flight on foot. He was one kill away from shift shaping and becoming a bat or cat or wolf. He was one his way to make that kill for dinner, after desert of course.

"I'm hungry," Keli said like always. There were packs of plasma in the fridge but she didn't want to ruin her meal. She was hot to hear about the fire that claimed Daniel before she could get to him. Kristine torched the apartment and corpses before she left them.

"Aren't you always!" Tosha said in the sharp tone of a friend who no longer wants to be a friend. Headlights in the driveway paused the ensuing argument.

"The strippers are here!" Kamala cheered when she peeped out the window. She waited until they reached the door and let three beefy dancers in.

"Yay!" Tosha sang and clapped as she checked them out. Not the way most of their patrons did.

"I thought you said a man booked us?" The biggest of the three whined and rolled his eyes.

"You better chill, girl!" another snapped and threw in, "Man up!"

"Hey, ladies. Y'all ready for the show?" the last man said. He was the least effeminate of the three but birds of a feather wear feather boas together.

"We are!" Keli snarled. She would have set it off on the spot if Kamala didn't intervene.

"Not here. Let's go up to the Boom Boom Room," Kamala suggested and led the way. She put a little extra wiggle in her walk but the three men didn't look.

"Kinky!" the big one gushed when they entered the all red room. The nonporous walls and floors made clean up easy and it was about to get messy.

"Well, let's get to it!" the other said and the room exploded in violence.

*****

"Grrrr, grrrr, grrr...huh?" Janice growled as she fed between a girl's legs. She ate plenty of pussy but was currently sucking blood from her femoral artery.

"What's wrong?" her meal asked when she abruptly stopped. She was more worried about the money for meth she was promised in exchange for letting the vampire drink her blood.

"Nothing. Go!" she demanded and stood just as the Dark Prince walked into her trailer.

"Just in time for dinner, I see," Prince said and smiled with his platinum fangs.

"Another one? Cool! Fifty bucks," the junkie said and extended her hand to get paid. Instead, Prince grabbed her head and twisted so far, she could now watch her own back.

"You didn't have to do that," Janice griped and flipped her blonde hair out of her face.

"I know. I wanted to," he said and moved closer. "You knew I was coming didn't you?"

"Yes," she said and lifted her shirt over her head. Prince locked on to her luscious breast while she stepped out of her shorts. "I was hoping we could get along. That's why I came to your show."

"Why did you leave?" he asked as she lowered herself in front of him.

"Cuz you had three thirsty vampires with you. I knew you felt me, so I came here and waited," she replied. Her end of the conversation ended when she wrapped her thin lips around his thick dick.

Prince looked around the trailer and knew why she lived here. She was surrounded by disposable people the world wouldn't miss. Janice had a rotation of addicts she could feed on without killing. When she did go too far or drink too much, no one would know. No one would care since people like these went missing all the time.

"Whoa!" Prince grunted while the woman worked her magic. She couldn't pull a rabbit out of a hat but sucked him so well, he took a seat on the old sofa.

"Can I ride it?" she asked as if her life depended upon pleasing said him. It did since the biggest killer of vampires is other vampires. Next was Kristine Musa.

"You sure can," Prince said and helped her up. She helped her own campaign when she stood flat-footed on his thighs and lowered herself down onto the dick. Prince was impressed when she twerked on the tip of dick before easing it inside her cramped box.

"I see you like!" Janice cheered and squeezed. Other vampires had come through town and got the same routine. She didn't need an answer, so she popped a titty in his mouth and kept on working.

Prince enjoyed the ride for a while before flipping her over on her back and took control. He lifted her legs by both ankles with one hand and gave her a smooth pounding. She tried to put it on him but he flipped the script and put it on her. Janice let out a whimper and bust a creamy nut all over his dick.

Prince was right behind her and snatched out at the last second and offered her a drink. She gladly gulped him down to prove her worth to him. A vampire freak on the side is worth its weight in blood."

So, do we have an understanding?" she asked between kisses and licks on his dick.

"We do," Prince agreed. He still extended his claws and beheaded her with a quick swipe. "We both understand that only the strong survive."

Prince took what remained of Ella when he left the trailer. He dropped the body and head along the way, knowing the sun would dispose of them when it rose. He moved swiftly through the night with his feet barely touching the ground. His new powers kicked in and he took flight. Literally as he turned into a bat and began to fly.

He fluttered around enjoying his newfound skill then rushed home.

"Uh oh," Prince said when he literally landed in his backyard. He always could sense any vampires in his immediate area. He sensed the same vampire energy coming from the house, but something was different. He slowly walked inside and saw for himself.

The house was ransacked and completely covered in blood. He expected to only see one of the girls left and he was right. It just wasn't the one he expected to see.

"You?" Prince winced when he saw the soul survivor sitting on the sofa in a room littered with body parts.

"Yeah, I decided to go solo." Kamala sighed. Prince peered inside her mind and watched the nights events play out in her mind.

"Well, let's get to it," the stripper said to start the show.

"Let's!" Keli agreed and flew across the room at Tosha in a blur. The largest of the three Beefcakes let out a high-pitched scream when the two vampires bared their fangs in mutual combat.

The men made a run for it as Keli and Tosha began a fight to the death. They clawed and bit at each other and painted the red room even redder. Tosha took a chunk of Keli's cheek and spit it aside. Keli nearly disemboweled Tosha with her claws.

"Oh no, you don't!" Kamala said and went after the strippers. She paralyzed the closest one with a quick jab through his spine. She leapt over him and caught the largest one just as he reached the door. He grabbed the doorknob so tightly, Kamala couldn't dislodge him. Instead, she chopped him off at the wrist and pulled him away.

"Un uh. Come on!" the remaining man said and put up his dukes. "I used to be all state in wrestling!"

"Well, I'm a whole vampire," Kamala laughed and attacked him, too. He intended to put up a fight but it wasn't much of a fight. Kamala scooped him and slammed him on the ceiling first. Then to the ground hard enough to crack the hardwood floors and his back. "Now you a whole snack!"

Tosha and Keli were locked in battle upstairs while Kamala fed. She drank from the large man by the door and the one on the floor but saved the paralyzed man for later.

The rumbling upstairs came to an abrupt end when one of the vampires lost their life for a second time. There would be no more lives in this life for them. Kamala marched up the stairs to confront the winner before she could recover.

"I didn't expect to see you," she told a bloody and battered Keli.

"Bring me one of them. Or plasma," she pleaded. She won the battle but barely and was almost as close to death as the dead girl beside her. She needed blood to recover or she would die, too.

"Nah," Kamala said and clamped down on her throat. She bit down with all her might until her jaws closed tightly together. What little blood that remained gushed on the floor in front of her.

"I saved you some!" Kamala offered and smiled.

"Wow," Prince said and just shook his head. He pulled the paralyzed man up by his neck, then pulled the head back and bit into his jugular. The man was numb from the shock of what he saw and now what he was going through. Luckily, the light began to fade as he slipped away.

"You're going to clean this shit up!" he barked and marched off.

*****

"Oh my God! Oh my God! Did you hear? Of course, you heard! Oh my God!" Meechie fussed as he rushed inside the house.

"Heard what?" Prince asked groggily since he just awoke from his slumber. It was genuine since he had a very busy night. "Where are the girls? They with you?"

"I'm sorry, bruh," he moaned and took a seat. He frowned from the dampness of the sofa. It was a big improvement from how it looked a few hours ago before Kamala cleaned it.

"What?" Prince asked quite believably. As if he couldn't read minds or didn't already know what happened.

"They gone, man. Car wreck," Meech said with his voice cracking with sorrow.

"Say what?" he asked in preparation for a movie roll. He went for an Oscar when he rushed up to the girls bedrooms and calling their names. Tosha! Keli! Kamala!"

"They gone, bruh. Their car hit an embankment this morning. Burst into flames. They gone," he repeated.

Of course, Prince already knew this since he was the one who staged the accident just before dawn. He made love to the lone survivor, Kamala one last time, then killed her, too. What new powers he gained from absorbing the three were yet to be determined. He would need them since he sensed that Butta would return soon. He was going to need everything he had and more to defeat him once and for all.

"Well, make sure their families get whatever they had coming. Should be plenty since their album is number one," Prince advised. They both stood to make millions from the girls album if they were dead or alive.

"I have some more girls. A little rough around the edges..." Meech offered in hopes Prince could or would make them over like he did Tosha, Kamala and Keli.

"Nah, no more girl groups. I think I'm ready for a feature film. Hook it up," Prince said and stood once more.

"Um, okay. Yeah! I got you, man," he said after Prince as he walked away and went upstairs.

CHAPTER 15

"This should have worked! Why didn't this work!" Kristine fussed as she went over her formula, line by line and it was thousands of lines. She had run every test known to man and vampire on Daniel's blood and it was human. Not a trace of the virus that turns people into the undead. She repeated her test on the vial of known vampire blood and it killed it dead. There was now just one more vial of pure vampire blood courtesy of the Dark Prince.

"This should have worked!" she demanded once more. She had been cooped up in her Atlanta hotel for over a week doing nothing more than working on the cure. Pure frustrated desperation led her to pull up the rarely used video chat on the computer. She made sure she was fully dressed before she did. The video request was answered right away.

"What took you so long?" Prince asked with an arrogant laugh that made Kristine click right back off.

"Shit! Shit! Shit!" she fussed and cussed since she knew she needed him. The last week was spent going around in circles and she was no closer to solving the riddle. She let out a deep sigh and clicked the Dark Prince right back into her life.

"Yes?" he asked but turned down the hubris. Just a little because not much could be done with the sly smirk on his face. She would live with it so she moved on.

"I need your help," she blurted since it was the only way to get it out. Asking him to help her find a cure for himself was like asking the devil how to get to paradise.

"Yeah, you look a little uptight. Okay, take your middle finger and make small circles around your clitoris. Then—"

"Not with that!" she shrieked from embarrassment. Especially since that was the one distraction she did allow herself since she turned recluse. "I can take care of that very well. Thank you very much!"

"The formula, I assume. I guess you got ahold to one of these amateurs running around here," he said.

"Something like that and it doesn't work! He still died!" she shouted in frustration.

"Meet me at S and S Chicken and Waffles. You know the place? On Peachtree. On the patio in case you try some funny business," Prince laughed like he was afraid of her. He chose an open area so she wouldn't be afraid of him. Unnecessary since she wasn't afraid of anything. The type of gallantry that can work for or against a person.

"I'm not meeting you anywhere!" Kristine spat indignantly. She opened her mouth to say more, but the screen went dead. "Did he hang up? Ugh!"

"Wait for it," Prince chuckled and watched his screen. A second later, the disheveled vampire hunter clicked back on. "Yes?"

"Okay. I'll meet you. S and S on Peachtree. Give me ten minutes," she conceded.

"Let's make it an hour. So you can make yourself presentable," Prince said with that arrogant smile pasted on his handsome face.

"No, he didn't!" Kristine said as she stood from her computer. She caught a glimpse of herself with her hair all over her head and looking a mess overall. Her eyes had dark bags under them and her thick lips looked dry and cracked.

"Hmph!" she huffed. That didn't mean he was right, but she still rushed into her bathroom and under the shower. Kristine bathed and groomed herself. She shaved her long legs then moved up to her pubes. Her underarms were last and she stepped out feeling refreshed. The water curled her naturally curly hair a little more. She tucked it into a bun and picked out something to wear.

"Um, this is not a date!" she scolded herself and put the sexy dress she selected back on the rack. A pair of khaki pants got the call along with a pair of comfortable flats. Last was a polo type shirt to play down her big breast. It was a good idea but her nipples still poked out in defiant anticipation. "Down, girls!"

Kristine grabbed her laptop with her formula and findings and rushed towards the door. She stopped just short of leaving and turned back. She picked up a syringe of her solution and headed back out. She didn't have to put her pistol in her purse since she kept it in her purse at all times. A few minutes later, she arrived at the popular eatery.

"Almost forgot you were a rapper," she said when she saw the group of groupies fluttering around like tattooed butterflies. It butterflies wore booty shorts that is. Prince signed autographs on napkins and titties. He felt her presence and lifted his head as she crossed the street towards him.

Enough, Prince suggested and the girls dispersed immediately. He waited as Kristine navigated through the interior of the restaurant and made her way out onto the patio.

"As salaamu alaykum," he greeted and stood. He pulled her chair like a perfect gentleman and allowed her to sit.

"Wa alaykum as salaam. Why do you greet me in Arabic?" she wondered.

"Your name. It's Arabic. Musa is the name of—" he began until she jumped in.

"The prophet Moses. Peace be upon him. Did you know him?" she answered and asked.

"No, I'm not quite that old!" he laughed and showed another side of him. The genuine charm he once possessed when he was human.

"How old are you?" she asked and guessed early twenties in her head.

"Twenty-one forever, plus fifty something human years. So no, I didn't know Moses but I did know Doctor Martin Luther King," he said with a pride she could feel from across the table. She knew the name but wasn't American, so it didn't hold the same weight as a prophet. Still she listened as he relayed the events of his seventy plus years on the planet.

"Haiti has always been a hotbed of vampire activity. I've been there several times. There's an extremely dangerous and very elusive vampire there named—"

"Katrina. Yes, I know her very well. She is dead," Prince jumped in.

"She is!" Kristine shouted in awe. "How? She was so powerful!"

"A vampire more powerful than her came along. He came for me too in Cleveland," he said slowly and let her catch up.

"He's the one I injected!" she recalled.

"He's the one who nearly killed you!" Prince reminded. He commenced to scolding her like a big brother would.

"I nearly killed him, as well! I could have changed him back," she shot back. "If my formula had worked. Why won't it work?"

"It works. I'm sure you've tried it in your lab. With my blood?" he asked.

"And it works. But when I try on a real vampire, they die," she whined.

"That's because they don't want it to work. They have to repent in their soul before it will work," he explained. Over the years, many of the vampires he killed had willingly given in. "They knew their souls were doomed to hell if they didn't repent."

"Interesting," she nodded and retrieved the syringe from her purse. "Let's try it. Repent, and let me inject you."

"Nah. I'm having too much fun!" Prince laughed. He wouldn't admit to how many times he wished he could be normal again. "Besides, Butta is coming back. I have to be ready."

"If he killed Katrina he'll kill you, too!" she urged like she cared. She heard it, too, but didn't try to clean it up. The man across the table from her was gorgeous. She wouldn't mind him being human not one bit.

"I'll be okay. I'm pretty powerful myself," Prince said with some of that arrogance coming back. "Why don't you let me turn you? Hang out with me for a couple centuries. You can reverse it any time you like because it works. Your solution works!"

"And kill people for food? Leave littered corpse for little girls to find when they come home from school?" Kristine asked. A single tear dropped from her eye, but she angrily knocked it away before it could run down her lovely face.

"Think about it. Butta is coming for you, too. Probably first!" Prince reminded and stood. He stifled a smile when she shot a glance down at his crotch.

"And I'll finish what I started when he does!" she shot back defiantly and stood. She stifled a blush at the sexy scan he ran over her body. He made her feel like a woman. They locked eyes for a full minute before speaking again.

Prince could have easily went inside of her head but didn't need to. Kristine was a woman and her feelings were written all over her face.

"Well, I'll see you later," Prince stated as a fact.

"You will," Kristine agreed. She had no doubt she would see him again. Prince was right about that but he was about something else, as well. Butta was coming and he was coming for her first.

CHAPTER 16

"I'm back!" Butta sang when his plane began to descend in Atlanta. He was feeling stronger and knew it was time to take care of the Dark Prince once and for all. He had plans for this so-called vampire hunter who almost killed him. He could still feel the effects of the silver she shot him up with.

Butta was pretty well off too from his own career as a rapper. Plus, he was a vampire and could do anything he wanted to. That included making people give him money if they wanted to or not. Even that had been a little cloudy after Kristine injected him with whatever she injected him with. He still had trouble getting into people's head to read their thoughts. It was like someone channel surfing with images flicking by.

He knew his strength came from finding and killing other vampires. If he couldn't find some, he would just turn some. He planned to pay Janice a visit in South Carolina, but she wasn't alive.

"Well, hello," a woman greeted and smiled when the plane came to a stop at the gate. Butta had reached over her to retrieve his bag from the overhead bin and found his body pressed against her backside.

"Hello there, yourself," he smiled back and commanded his body to erect an erection.

"Ooh lala!" she giggled when she felt the wood throbbing against her. Butta noticed the scarf tied around her neck and wondered if it was a hickie or bite marks from a vampire.

"You're coming with me, young lady," he invited. She gave a girlish giggle and followed him off the plane.

"Mica," she introduced so he wouldn't have to call her young lady. She was quite impressed when they reached the car he kept in the long-term lot. "Ooh lala!"

"You think that's something, look at this," he said and leaned back to whip out the wood.

"It is nice!" she marveled and leaned over. Her head bobbed as he pulled up to the cashier to pay for his parking.

"Two hundred, oh my!" the woman gasped when she saw the blowjob in motion. Butta just laughed and handed over his credit card. She ran the card and passed it and the receipt back while trying not to see what was going on in the front seat. The slurps and gagged made that hard to do.

"Thank you," he chuckled and pulled away. He barely made it to 285 before Mica got him off. She leaned back for the trip into the city.

Butta kept a mansion in the Hollywood hills when he was on the West coast and another in the Hamptons when he was in New York. When in Atlanta he kept a midtown loft.

"I'll just bring my bag," Mica suggested when they arrived. Just in case the handsome older man wanted her to stay for a while.

"Sure, cuz you're not going anywhere anytime soon," he said and led her inside. He wasted no time and led her straight to his room. He set the tone and began to undress.

Mica followed suite and it was obvious she liked an audience. She made a big show of removing her blouse and traced her lacy bra with manicured fingers. She reached around and unhooked her bra and set the picture perfect breast free. They were so firm they didn't budge when she removed the bra. He knew they were new when she looked down and admired them as well. Butta knew something was wrong when she left her scarf off.

"Let's see what you working with," Butta said and squinted. He expected to see some hickies or even a vampire bite. What he didn't expect to see was the Adam's Apple that meant she was a he. "What the—"

"You knew," Ella said and twisted his lips. Butta shot his glance down to lump in his panties.

"Knew what? You're not a girl?" he demanded hotly.

"Yes. I am a girl. I'm in transition. Got the top done. All I need now is the bottom," he said calmly. A low growl emitted from Butta as the man stepped out of his panties.

"You're a boy?" Butta exploded and snatched him off his feet by his throat. He lifted him up and bit his whole package complexly off. He spit it aside and slammed him down to the floor. The plan to turn him went out the window and Butta just watched him bleed out. He stuffed his stuff back in his mouth and drug him back out to his car.

Butta put what was left of him, or her now, into his trunk and went back into the night. He still needed to feed and still needed to turn another vampire for strength since he was here for a showdown with the Dark Prince. He drove over to the hoe stroll on Metropolitan Avenue and dropped off his trash while picking up two teenaged prostitutes. Young girls who were too good to work fast food, so they slung ass for fast cash. Ironically, they posted up in the parking lot of a Mrs Winners with a "Help Wanted" sign in the window.

"Come. Both of you!" Butta ordered after dumping the body in the dumpster.

"A hunnid each!" the head hoe in charge demanded before they budged. She was the spokes-hoe for the both of them.

"How about two hunnid each?" Butta asked and flashed that sexy cash. That got their fat asses in the car quicker than a magic trick to turn this trick. A few hours later, they were both thoroughly fucked and turning into vampires. Butta fucked them and sucked them before making them drink his blood. He put them in a room to ferment until they were ripe.

*****

Meanwhile, the lines between villain and vigilante had blurred when Prince went to feed. A pedophile pedagogue with a penchant for pederasty had just been acquitted of several counts against his pupils.

The man opted for a bench trial and the judge sided with his defense of "it wasn't me" over twenty victims going back twenty years. This didn't sit well with Prince, so he decided to take matters into his own hands.

No one has time to figure out what the judge was thinking, so he went to him on a visit and let him explain himself for dinner. Then he would stop and see the teacher for desert.

The judge was sitting in his den enjoying a movie when Prince eased in behind. He grimaced at the filth on the screen and saw he had company beside him.

"Sho nuff!" Prince cheered at his good fortune. He lucked out and got the chance to kill two birds with one stone when he saw who was next to him. "Judge Judy and the teacher of the year!"

"Who are you! What are you doing in my house!" the judge demanded indignantly, despite the kiddie porn on the screen.

"First things first," the uninvited guest replied and threw a heavy ashtray through the flat screen mounted on the wall.

"I think I should go," the teacher said and stood to excuse himself.

"You should," Prince agreed a lopped his head completely off with his claws. It flipped in the air until he caught it.

"Oh my!" the judge declared like a southern belle when the vampire lifted the head to his mouth and drank the blood like a chalice.

"You don't mind watching children engaged in sex acts on a 80-inch screen but this offends you?" Prince asked and tossed the head aside like an empty coconut.

The old man nodded to himself and then at his decision to go for his gun. Prince shrugged and watched him scramble to get it and make sure it was loaded. He pointed and pulled the trigger, but it clicked harmlessly.

"Safety," Prince advised helpfully.

"Oh, yeah!" the judge agreed and took the safety off. He tried again and this time the trusty revolver pumped six rounds into Prince's torso. He took a step forward with every shot and stood right over the man.

"Care to reload?" Prince laughed down at him.

"What are you?" the man demanded when the same bullets he just pumped into him began to pop back out and hit the floor.

"Your judge!" he said and found the man guilty. He clamped his fangs deep into his throat and drank his fill. He tossed him on top of his friend and left them both right there. The police could explain this one however they liked when they were found. Come to find out, they were finding a lot of vampire deaths around the city as of late. Kristine was right about vampires in Atlanta. She just didn't know how right she was.

CHAPTER 17

"What do we have?" Kristine asked when she arrived at the morgue after an unusual violent night in the violent city. If Martin Luther King had any idea what would come of his people, he might not have died for the cause.

"You must be Miss Musa," a new coroner asked and checked her out. He would have been handsome if not for the greedy look in his eyes as he looked her up and down.

"Who are you? Where is Doctor Ford?" she asked hotly. She usually dressed down to avoid being looked at the way he was looking at her right now.

"Retired. Mental breakdown if you ask me," he shrugged, then continued. "Now I know we have had some mutilations, but don't come in here with none of that vampire shit!"

"Okay. What mutilations came in recently?" she asked with a smirk. She knew she would make a believer out of this one just like she did the last. Vampires were very real and proved themselves.

"This was found in a dumpster this morning," he said and pulled the drawer out. He pulled the sheet away and revealed what was left of Mica.

"Oh?" she reeled from the perfect breast under the Adam's Apple. The sight of his missing meat didn't give her any pause. "Was it found?"

"In his mouth. I'm pretty sure the semen in his belly didn't come from it," he said and cracked up. "Get it? Come, cum, from him?"

"Got it. Not funny," she said and leaned in to get a closer look at the bite marks where his genitals once lived.

The doctor couldn't resist looking at the round ass in front of him. He traced her panty lines between her legs and had to cop a feel. Kristine frowned in confusion at what felt like a hand groping her bottom. She reacted when she realized that was exactly what it was.

"Haya!" she shouted and did a 360 spin and slapped a spark out of his cheek.

"Feisty!" he cheered and cheesed as he felt the welts rising on his cheek. She glanced down and saw an erection bulging in his pants.

"Touch me again and—" she began to threaten but he interrupted since he heard it all before.

"Report me? Sue me? Cry? Hash tag me, too? What, you'll kill me?" he laughed.

"No, but you'll wish you were dead. I promise you that!" she shot back. She was almost as angry with herself at the thought that popped into her head. For some reason, she thought about telling Prince about the assault.

"Yeah, yeah," he laughed and waved it off. She decided she would tell Prince as he went on to show her the other bodies with bite marks on various parts of their bodies. It confirmed her suspicions that there were multiple vampires in this city.

*****

"Stop. I'm good," Prince said and pressed pause on the backstage blowjob he was receiving.

"Did I do something wrong?" the groupie whined and pouted. She had won out over the legion of girls vying for his attention. Prince was relieved by the knock on the door and stood up to answer it. He tucked the wood away and went to pull it open.

"Sup, shawty," Prince greeted when Meech met him in his dressing room. He booked several shows around the city to give the fans a peep at their latest idol. The girl scampered off as he came in.

"Sup," he greeted back. It was clear he was still pretty bummed out about losing Tosha, Kamala and Keli in one fell swoop. A glance inside his mind proved what was on his face.

"I know, bruh. I miss 'em, too. I'll dedicate tonight's show in their honor," Prince said. It was the least he could do since he was to blame for corrupting the girls. One could argue that the corruption was already in them since every person contains, or has the potential for three kinds of souls.

First, there's the soul that commands evil. The lower-based self that chases lust and desires. Then comes the self-reproaching self that knows the difference between wrong and right, good and evil. It strives to do good but can occasionally fall short. It is repentant if or when that happens. Last is the soul that is in complete rest and satisfaction. It's content with the limits of it's Lord and wouldn't go any where near disobedience.

"Do that. Can you shout out Angela? She's out there, too," Meechie asked.

"Sure," he said and stood. He realized his manager was his only friend and there wasn't much he wouldn't do to please him.

Prince walked out on stage and the crowd erupted. That was the reason he became a performer, but it seemed to have lost a little of its lore. Until the music started, that is and he began to do what he did best. He launched into a mixed medley of his entire repertoire.

Halfway through he noticed a flamboyant vampire come in with four newly turned vampires by his side. He was one of the strays who got away when the Princesses died. Each of them had been secretly turning new vampires so they could gain more strength for their solo careers. Each left at least one when they died and Lil Zag was one of them.

He was a wannabe rapper Kamala met backstage at a show. She infected him with their virus and sent him home to die so she could go kill him again. Only she died before she got the chance. Now he turned a few girls so he could have an entourage just like his favorite rapper on the stage right.

Prince peeped inside his mind and mentally jotted his address down before someone else waltzed in and demanded his attention.

The show may have been dedicated to the girls when it began but the remaining half was all for Kristine.

She dressed to impress herself mainly but knew the Dark Prince would appreciate the beige legs under the short red dress. They went well with the mound of cleavage protruding from the top of her low cut blouse.

Prince usually treated his audience to an encore, but tonight he had other plans. He rapped up his set with an acappella freestyle and dropped the mic. His hypnosis cleared a path as he exited the stage and made his way over to her table.

"Bravo," Kristine clapped. She wasn't exactly sure why she was here, but here she was. Prince cheated and went inside her mind and saw she didn't have an answer to the question that was on his mind, as well.

"You like?" he asked even though he got the answer to that while he was in her head. What he did gleam was the heat she felt about being felt up by the medical examiner. He made up his own mind not to read hers again or impose his will through hypnosis.

"I actually did! I'm more of a reggae gal, but you're okay," she admitted and smiled.

"Do you think you'll be able to still do it once I turn you back into a human?"

"Oh, I'm very much human now. Human, plus," he laughed and she laughed along with him. It set off a playful banter that lasted an hour. She even confided in him about being molested at the morgue.

"Guess I should go," Kristine said and stood.

"Okay. I'll see you in your dreams," Prince said and stood, as well.

"I doubt that, but come on with it," she dared and sashayed out of the club. She didn't need any special powers to know her shapely ass had an audience all the way out of the club. The other rapper/vampire rushed over as soon as she left his side.

"That was dope!" Lil Zag said and held up his hand for a pound. Prince frowned at him and his vampire groupies by his side.

"Are you the one leaving your empties on the street?" Prince wanted to know. He knew the key to survival is to move in silence and violence. This flamboyant guy dressed like a peacock obviously didn't catch that class.

"It's just food. Fast food. Take out," three of his girls said while the last one nodded.

"You're right! So let's go eat!" Prince cheered. "I have a four hundred pound man at my house right now. You all are invited!"

The group made their way over to Prince's house in a two-car caravan. He led them inside and up to the Boom Boom Room. Once they were all in, he locked the door behind him.

"Where's our food?" one of the girls whined when she realized the room was empty beside them.

"There is no food!" Lil Zag snapped when he got it. To his credit, he didn't go out without a fight. It wasn't much of a fight, but a fight none the less.

"You are the food!" Prince said and transformed into a large wolf. He nearly bit Lil Zag into two with his first bite. He left him to deal with the massive injury while he literally ate the four girls alive. He was an animal while ripping the vampires to shreds.

Even Prince was surprised at the carnage once his feeding frenzy subsided. There wasn't enough parts of the five left to make one by the time he transformed back into a man. It made clean up easy since there was less to put into his crematorium. Once the walls and floors were hosed clean, the room was as good as new.

Prince was too and let out a mighty roar as a surge of energy filled his body. The neighborhood dogs howled back in reply to his howl. He had reached a new milestone in the vampire world.

"Now, where is Butta?" Prince snarled. He was ready to rid the
world of his only competition but still had a couple errands to run
before dawn.

CHAPTER 18

Kristine tossed turned in her bed in search of sleep. She couldn't decide if she was hot or cold and alternated between pulling her sheets onto her body or kicking them away. She stripped away the confines of underwear and tried to relax. She would never admit how worked up Prince had her.

It finally looked like slumber would come as a gentle fog entered her room. It seemed to actually touch her as it rolled over her body. She kicked the sheets away once more and enjoyed the feel of the breeze on her legs. Her legs spread in hopes the wind would flow in that direction.

"Mmm!" Kristine moaned when the wind changed directions. It nibbled at the back of her knee before licking its way up her thigh. She felt a flush of juice gathering in her juice box hoping the wind would lick her there, as well.

It did and lifted her whole body off the bed. Kristine pulled her legs apart and thrashed as a whirlwind whipped around her pearl tongue. It darted in and out of her and caused her lonely vagina to throb.

"You're gonna make me fucking cum!" she shouted at the wind but the wind didn't let up. It kept doing what it was doing like it dared her to come.

Kristine lost that dare when her whole body shook and shivered from the most intense orgasm she ever had. The wind didn't let up though, it kept right on blowing until another orgasm shook the room.

She willed the wind to get hard and reached down to guide it inside of her. That took a minute since it felt so good to rub its big mushroom shaped head in between her slippery lips.

"Mmmm, ssss," she moaned and hissed as the wind sank slowly inside of her. It had a gentle stroke at first like any calm before any storm. It began to pick up strength in the hot pussy just like a hurricane does over the warm Gulf of Mexico.

Kristine came once again when an orgasm snuck up on her. The wind had a tongue and slid it into her mouth. She literally sucked it like she was giving it head as it stroked her. Stroked her in rhythm with a far away beat that she couldn't hear but damn sure felt.

"Oh, you gonna just keep making me cum, huh?" she asked and answered herself when she came again. She felt the puddle of juice pooling under her but didn't mind. She needed to change her sheets anyway, even through she just put them on that morning. She could think of every excuse in the book on behalf of that good stroking wind. She would lie in a court of law on its behalf by the time she came again.

"Go on. Come on," she urged when the wind grew choppy like any man would when he was about to come. She squeezed her hot back and encouraged it to come.

The wind let out a howl of its own and plunged to the bottom of her well. She could feel it pulsate and throb as it pumped her full of wind. She felt it gently kiss her lips, neck, breast, and stomach before leaving through the same window it came in.

"Mmmm," she moaned once and rolled over on her side. Hours past as quickly as minutes and her alarm clock began to ring. She groaned and rolled out of bed to begin her busy day. That started with a tinkle on the toilet before stepping into the shower.

"That was some dream!" she said in amazement when she felt a gentle soreness between her legs. She had never rubbed herself raw in any of the times she rubbed one out for herself.

"Okay, pretty girl. Let's see what the day brings," she told her reflection in the mirror. Her pleasant smile slowly turned down when she noticed an anomaly on her neck. She pushed her curls aside and leaned in for a closer look.

Kristine wore a full-fledged frown when she saw the two holes, perfectly aligned with her jugular vein. She was sure it was the steam from the shower, so she wiped the mirror dry with her towel, but the holes didn't go away.

Her phone barley rang, so she barely answered. This time she knew exactly who it was and rushed to answer it.

"Did you come here last night?" she demanded.

"Did I!" Prince laughed. "In fact, I came there twice. Not as many as you but—"

"You bit me?" she asked and touched her fingers to the holes in her neck.

"Had to. I had to get a taste. Well, another taste," Prince said. He could hear her blushing over the phone and cracked up.

Kristine knew the bite was next to harmless but now she could easily be turned if she drank his blood. There was still a full vial of it in her fridge. She had no intention on doing that but wondered if that applied to him cumming inside of her.

"I doubt that," he answered to her thought. Only because it boomed out of her head, so he didn't have to go inside.

"Wow! I, you..." Kristine fussed but couldn't find words. She knew vampires can't enter a home without being invited and shook her head at her almost tacit invitation. "Ugh!"

"See you later, babes," Prince laughed even though she had already hung up. She may not have heard him but he knew she felt him.

******

"Here we go," Kristine said to pump herself up when she reached the morgue. With the uptick in vampire activity lately, she had no reason to believe it would stop.

"Miss Musa, I presume?" yet another medical examiner greeted when she walked in.

"Yes, and you are?" she asked and looked around for Mr. Touchy-Feely.

"Drawer eleven," he answered to the question she didn't ask, then the one she did.

"I'm Doctor Stevenson. The new, new medical examiner."

"Drawer eleven?" Kristine asked as she made her way over. By now, she was very much familiar with the layout of this and many morgues around the world.

"Eleven," he repeated and squinted at the scarf around her neck.

"Oh my!" she said with a mouthful of mirth when she saw the previous coroner stretched out on his back. "Where are his hands?"

"Your guess is as good as mine," he replied and studied her as closely as she studied the corpse.

She expected to see bite marks on his neck but didn't. She could tell from the bruising and awkward angle that the cause of death was a broken neck. There were no outward signs of a vampire attack but she knew a vampire did it. In fact, she knew exactly which vampire did after venting to Prince about the grope. A slight smirk ended her examination of the man and she slid the drawer back in.

"Any unusual bodies turn up overnight?" Kristine asked and looked around.

"Young black men dead at the hands of other black men is unusual in itself," he replied.

"Indeed," she agreed. "I meant unexplained deaths. Gory, blood letting."

"You mean vampires?" the doctor asked knowingly.

"They're real!" she shot back in frustration. She had finally got one to believe and he quit on her. Now she had to start all over again.

"Oh, I know. Something tells me you know a little better than I," he said and nodded at her neck.

"I beg your pardon! My boyfriend likes to leave passion marks, not bite marks!" she shot back. There was a brief silence while he decided if he believed her or not. His head began to nod and eased the tension.

"Only one. Something changed?" he said of the sudden down tick in deaths. Neither knew that Prince personally disposed of the five vampires who caused much of the carnage. There were two more stragglers who had yet to be discovered.

And then there was Butta.

*****

"I can feel youuuuuu," Butta sang to himself as he perched in the VIP section of a nightclub. He was on the hunt for his supper when he felt the unmistakable essence of another vampire in his midst.

He scanned the dimly lit confines of the club and locked eyes with a young woman as she approached. She had worked in the club scene until a backstage encounter with Tosha during a show. She turned the bisexual into a trisexual when she seduced her in a coat closet. Tosha turned her into a vampire with plans to absorb her powers. She never made it and now the woman roamed the city in search of food.

"Butta," Butta greeted and stood like a gentleman when she reached his table.

"Clarissa," she said and watched him kiss her hand. He pressed his lips firmly against the veins on the back of her hand and felt the blood coursing below.

"You're new," he ascertained from her smell, taste, and demeanor.

"A few weeks old. Trying to get older, if you'll let me?" she asked. She had done her homework once she accepted what was wrong with her.

Clarissa awoke from the dead two days after her encounter with Tosha and couldn't eat. She had an insatiable thirst that water, juice or wine wouldn't quench. It wasn't until she bit her purring cat that she began to understand. She did her research and realized she was a vampire.

"I could," he said and inspected her once over. Every vampire needs a companion to ride out eternity with. Mortals just didn't fit the bill since they had a habit of getting older and dying.

"It looks better without the clothes," she said and stood so he could get a better look. She would have removed her tiny dress on the spot if that helped her cause. It wasn't necessary when Butta began to nod in approval. She was one of those new model white girls who came with a fat booty and thick lips.

"Let's go!" he decided and stood as well. They plucked a girl from the bar on their way out like a ripe fruit. She would be their bottle of champagne to consummate their new union.

*****

"Are you okay, Jimmy?" Officer Butler asked his partner as they cruised the city in their police car. He had wanted to ask him for a week now since his behavior had become increasingly bizarre.

"Huh? Oh, yeah. I just..." he stammered since he was wondering what was wrong with him, as well.

His last clear moments were from a week ago when he moonlighted a security job at a concert. Prince and his Princesses were performing and he had backstage access. He couldn't believe his good fortune when one of the sexy singers sought to seduce him. She took him into an empty dressing room and put him in her empty mouth.

Jimmy winced now from the memory of her biting him on his dick. The next thing he recalled was waking up at home with his angry wife standing over him. Lipstick on a collar is hard enough to explain, so what could be said about a hickie on his dickie?

His strong will allowed him to fight the thirst growing inside of him. It was beginning to totally consume him and he wasn't sure how much longer he could hold out. If he didn't drink blood soon, he would die or revert back to human. The latter never happens because they all fall victim to the thirst.

"We can go back to the station if you're feeling well. You don't look well," he said seeing sweat pouring from his open pores.

"I'm fine," he insisted just as a call came in about an armed robbery in progress. He grabbed the radio and took the call, obligating his partner to press on.

Butler shook his head and whipped around to rush towards the crime scene. They arrived and hopped out just as the masked suspect rushed out with a bag of money in one hand and an obvious toy gun in the other.

Gun!" Butler shouted and got an instant erection. The white cop had sat back and watched his white cop's brother get free kills on black men all over the country and now it was his chance.

"It's not real!" Jimmy was saying before his partner lifted him up. The heavy 40-caliber slug caused a mist of blood to fill the air when they slammed into his torso. The sight and smell was too much for Jimmy to resist. He dropped his weapon and rushed over to the fallen teen. "What are you doing Jimmy? Jimmy!" Butler shouted, but his pleas fell on deaf ears. He could only watch in shock and horror as the partner he known for years ran over and slurped blood from the gunshot wounds. He switched between several of the holes until he settled on the one that paid out best.

The store security camera as well as the police body cams both caught the spectacular footage of a vampire feeding.

"Jimmy! Back away from the perp!" Butler screamed and pointed his service weapon at his face. Jimmy looked up, bared his fangs, and hissed. That was enough for him to gun him down, as well.

Jimmy rolled away from the victim when the gunshot wound slammed into his body.

"This is Officer Butler! I need assistance! Officer down!" He yelled into his walkie-talkie. He didn't know what to make of this strange scene, but then it got even stranger.

Jimmy hopped up to his feet and took off. He turned into a Blue Blur and tore off down the street. His partner could believe what he just witnessed. Lucky for him he got it all in his body Camp. Unlucky for the vampires trying to stay on the low, the store security camera got the same footage. Vampires were real and they now had it on video.

CHAPTER 19

"Did you see the news?" Kristine asked when Prince took her call. She finally had a reason to call and jumped all over it. She had started a couple of texts that never got sent off. The standard "hey, big head" and "wyd" text that chicks sent after dudes laid some really good pipe.

"Hey, big head," Prince laughed even though he knew the footage of the vampire cop drinking blood would be a problem. He knew every vampire in the country would come looking for the new meat. It was unnecessary heat that he did not need. The news footage was they were coming out and they were coming out.

"You're awfully calm about this!" She shot back. She should be happy to finally have confirmation and validation of her life's work, but knew this could be a problem as well.

"Because this may save me some gas," he said since he still planned to kill every vampire he came in contact with. There can only be one and he planned to be that one. He broke the awkward silence and changed the subject. "Can I come see you?"

"Can I cure you?" She shot back immediately.

"No," he said just as quickly.

"So no, then!" Kristine returned like a tennis volley. She sounded tough, but it didn't last long before she broke down and said "Okay."

"Okay, what?" Prince pressed.

"Okay, you can come, but no sex," she heard herself say. Even she heard the lust in her voice and she knew he heard it, too. She quickly hung up and tossed the phone aside.

Kristine had barely got under the steaming shower when she heard a knock on her door. She had left it unlocked, so he she didn't bother to rush. Once she finished bathing, she dried off and came out to find a vampire in her bed.

Kristine was a tough woman, a dangerous woman, but a woman nonetheless. She could have not ignored the way he made her feel when they were together or apart. That did not change what she had to do, but it will not be done tonight. He was still a vampire and he had to be cured or killed.

They locked eyes as she stepped out of the bathroom just as naked as he was lying on her bed. Their eyes parted ways so they could check out body parts. Prince couldn't decide which he liked better between the big beige breasts, capped with large brown nipples or the freshly shaved, plump pussy beneath the hard, flat stomach. Meanwhile, she locked in on his magnificent dick. It was already rock hard in anticipation of their reunion. She made a beeline over and immediately took him into her mouth. Prince watched for a moment before flipping it over so he could simultaneously return the favor.

"Mmmm," Kristine moaned when his tongue touched her pearl tongue. He parted her labia with his tongue and probed her insides. Minutes later, she shook with from what would be the first of many orgasms of the evening.

Prince was somewhat shocked when she took the lead and rode his face until another orgasm shook the room. She was still in control when she mounted his dick and took off in search of another nut. Once she found it, it was his turn to take over. Prince flipped Kristine onto her back and slowly slid back inside of her. They locked eyes as he slow stroked her soaked vagina. Eye contact only paused to twirl tongues in each other's mouth. He knew she was mortal and couldn't go all night like he could. She actually bought out of hint of mortality in him when an orgasm crept up on him. Christine noticed the change in his rhythm and wrapped her legs around his back so he couldn't escape. As much pleasure as he had gave her, the least she could do was give him a warm, tight space to come.

Prince bared his fangs and pumped her box full of little vampire babies. "A dang vampire," Kristine said and shook her head. He had her wrapped around his finger and she knew it.

"A dang mortal," he chuckled in reply because the feeling was as mutual as their last orgasm. They cuddled in the post orgasmic bliss and pondered separately over the same dilemma. Good and bad do not mix. One of them would have to change.

*****

Prince could feel the influx of vampires in his city. They came in droves with the wannabe vampires and vampires through enthusiasts in the response to the footage of the policeman drinking blood. Word soon began to spread about the impending showdown between the two alpha males. Vampires can communicate through telepathy and the meeting was set. A vampire coming out party.

Meanwhile, the vampire hunter had a dilemma of her own. She had to convince Prince to take her cure so they could be together. After days of debate, she made up her mind and took action. "Here's to everything!" she said and made a mock toast in the air, and poured the last vial of prince's blood in her mouth.

She knew what to expect next, so she laid in her soft bed to make a comfortable transition into being dead. Then she could wake up alive as a vampire. It would be the only way to convince Prince to let her turn him back into a mortal. Then they could live a normal life, and die a natural death.

"Argh!" Kristine gasped and realized death would not be an easy transition. Her back arched almost to the point of breaking. Death was on the way and it would not be easy. She writhed in agony for hours until sweet death swept through and saved her. It would be two days before she was reborn, so she was going to miss the big event.

*****

"Do you think he'll be there?" Clarissa asked they readied themselves for meeting. They did that by feeding on two women they kidnapped from the bus stop. The city of Atlanta had become a virtual ghost town once the vampire attack was blasted on every station.

"What?" Butta snapped. Not to the question, she asked but the one he pulled for her frontal lobe. She had no idea he had been reading her thoughts from day one.

He heard her loud and clear when she lusted over the Dark Prince when his latest video came on. He wasn't just another rapper since Butta knew he was his biggest threat.

"I said, do you think he will show?" she repeated with a soft smile and a milk mustache of blood.

"No, you think he will defeat me!" Butta growled. He was feeling stronger from feeding off the influx of new vampires. He knew Prince could as well and wanted to strike before he could.

"No, I—" Clarissa began until interrupted by a vicious swipe from Butta's sharp claws. Her head rolled away while her body stood in place for a moment until gravity pulled it down.

"There can be only one," he told the head when it came to rest in the corner.

Butta went on and finished off his meal then dressed to impress. The vampire affair was turning out to be a big event. Even civilians had gotten wind and flocked to the venue. Some wanted the honor of having a vampire feed on them so they could show off the bite marks like a tattoo. Many of them wanted to be turned so they, too, could rule the night.

A huge church that had been recently abandoned in favor of nightclubs and Netflix had been chosen as the venue. A circus like atmosphere surrounded the event. The CDC, FBI, DEA, and Atlanta police consulted on what they should do, or could do. They decided they couldn't do shit but sit back and see how it unfolds. Especially since the number one vampire hunter in the world wasn't answering her phone. It was feared she had been killed. The truth was far worse.

"After tonight, this city, this continent, this world will be mine!" Butta told himself and set out.

******

"Where are you? What are you up to?" Prince asked when Kristine's phone went to voicemail again. He thought about flying over to her apartment since he could fly but had plans to put in motion.

That many vampires in one place was something he couldn't pass up. He even planned to perform for the packed crowd. He was a rapper after all and rappers rap. It's what they do and he was one of the best who ever done it.

"I'm gonna raise the roof!" Prince said and let out a sinister laugh at his sinister plans. He made his way over to the church and was amazed at the turnout.

Street vendors hawked vampire t-shirts and fake fangs. Concession stands sold ruby red drinks that resembled fake blood. "Bite me" stations similar to old school kissing booths were set up all around the church.

"I knew it!" a fan shouted when Prince made his way through the crowd. He was by far the most famous vampire of the hundreds of vampires in attendance.

Prince could feel the kinetic vampire energy floating in the room like electric current. Most were weak, newly turned, with no vampire kills under their belts. That made it easy to spot Butta when he walked in before Prince took the stage. Both gladiators mixed and mingled for a few hours while opening acts opened the show. Dawn wasn't far off when the Dark Prince finally took the stage. His diamond and platinum fangs glistened and sparked under the bright stage lights.

"Are you ready for a show?" Prince growled through the mic. In return, the crowd lost their damn minds. Groupies bared their breast, while vampires bared their fangs.

Vampires were on the verge of going global and tonight was their coming out party. Prince was the best-known rapper in the world and would be their spokesman if he survived the upcoming battle.

"Are y'all ready to raise this muthafuckin' roof!" Prince demanded and they screamed back a resounding, "Hell yeah!"

That was good enough for the Dark Prince to launch into a vicious performance that even had Butta nodding his head. He was pleased to see the adulation the Dark Prince received since it would transfer to him once he killed him in front of all of these people.

The revolution would not be televised since phones and recording devices were strictly banned. Alarms and beeps alarmed and beeped through the crowd as dawn approached. No one was particularly concerned since this was a vampire party and a vampire party don't stop. If Prince wanted to party all night, all day and into next week, they would party with him.

"Now, for the main event," Prince said and nodded towards the light man. Prince took the liberty of setting up his show in advance. On cue, Meechie pressed a button and put the spotlight on Butta.

Meechie couldn't believe his only friend and client was a real vampire. It certainly explained a lot of things. Either way, he was down for the Dark Prince until the end.

"Bravo," Butta said with a slow clap as he made his way to the middle of the floor. He took his shirt off and took a battle stance with fangs and claws on the ready.

Prince was already shirtless from his performance and hopped from the stage all the way over to the middle of the floor. The civilians and newer vampires "oohed" and "aahed" at the supernatural display. He could hear most of them plotting on other vampires so they too could make leaps like that.

Prince flicked his hands and popped out his fangs like the Wolverine from the X-men. It got another reaction from the crowd that made Butta twist his lips. The music was cut and all attention was turned to the two men in the middle of the makeshift ring made of people and vampires as the battle got underway.

Butta wielded his long claws like twin machetes and swung at Prince. Prince allowed him to connect and open deep wounds in everything he touched.

"Un huh. In a bit of trouble, huh?" Butta gloated over his handy work. The words were barely out of his mouth before the wounds completely closed. All vampires have the ability to self heal, but not as quickly as he just did.

The sight got another round of "oohs" and "aahs" from the crowd but Butta was worried. He knew he couldn't heal as quickly on his best day and even less after Kristine had injected him with her solution. He felt sluggish and slower most days but recent kills had him feeling himself, even if he wasn't feeling like his old self.

"I do believe it's my turn," Prince asked and answered with a few swipes of his own. Butta's deep cuts he inflicted didn't heal instantly like his did.

Prince realized he could have easily killed the man but didn't. Not only did he want to punish the man, he had a point to make. A deterrent to all the wannabe vampires in attendance as well as all those to come.

"There can be only one," Butta grunted with defeat in his voice. This was the way it had to be even if it didn't go his way. He lunged with a blow that would have killed Prince, but Prince wasn't there.

"Close," Prince laughed from behind him. Butta was now very afraid. He'd only come across one other vampire who was this powerful in his life. He barely escaped with his life that time, but knew he wouldn't be so lucky this time.

Butta put on a good show with lunges and swipes but Prince's show was better as he moved like the matrix and went untouched. Several roosters in the church began to crow to announce the dawn. They too would fight to the death just like the combatants on the floor.

"It's time," Prince said with a reverence for his one time friend. Butta sighed and let out an acquiescent sigh. He lifted his his head as Prince turned into a wolf like creature and bit it completely off.

Prince was a blur of fur and fangs and claws as he rushed around the beheading and disemboweling vampires all over the room. He spared the civilians so they could relay the story of this morning. His slaughter led him right back onto the stage. He looked over a stunned Meech and gave a nod and final command.

"Raise the roof!" he said and looked up.

Meechie hit the button and the roof blew away. Sunlight rushed in and devoured the corpses of the dead or dying vampires. Prince was prepared to go as well since his last talk with Kristine.

She was right and he was a murdering monster. He would have gladly taken her cure if not for the legions of vampires left behind. He lured as many as he could in one place and set their wicked souls free. Her cure worked and she could do the rest.

In the process, he absorbed all of their powers. Hundreds of vampires at one time. It would prove or disprove his theory for once and for all. Prince closed his eyes and felt the heat and rays of the sun for the first time in decades. The room lit up in an orange glow from the burning vampires throughout the room. They all burned, except for Prince. His eyes opened as slowly as the smile spread on his face.

He looked up at the harmless sun and realized he had made it. He was now a day walker.

CHAPTER 20

"Come in!" Kristine called out in the reply to the knocking on her door. She already knew who it was from all the missed calls on her phone. That and vampires can feel other vampires.

"I am," Prince said and used his shoulder to unlock the front door. His heart sank when he felt her before he even saw her. Kristine was huddled in a corner of her bedroom looking crazy. "What did you do?"

"If you can't beat them..." she chuckled, then winced from a sharp hunger pain of thirst.

"Oh, baby. Why?" he moaned and came over. He felt her hot skin and knew what she needed. If she didn't get blood, she would die soon. He disappeared and reappeared in a blink of an eye with a pack of plasma he kept in a cooler in his trunk.

"No," she tried to resist when he pressed the packet to her mouth. Her fangs stretched out despite her protest. Prince pushed the pack against it and the fangs sank inside. Kristine was powerless against her own self and greedily sucked the pack dry. Prince rushed to get another and she drank her fill.

"Now why?" he demanded once she regained her composure. Her color had come back and her skin was cleared.

"Because, if you won't turn mortal for me, than I'll be a vampire! We can hunt people and kill them. Leave them for their daughters to find just like my mother!" she snapped. She fussed and cussed on for a while, but Prince heard her real reason loud and clear. She wanted to be with him.

"Okay," he tossed in when she paused to take a breath. It didn't register right away and her tirade continued.

"And then we can kill and drink babies blood and wait...what?" she asked when the words finally processed.

135

"I said okay. I'll take your cure. I am willing to change so it will work," he assured her. "You first and I'm right behind you."

"Come on then! You first, and then me!" he shot back and caused her to twist her lips dubiously.

"Mmhm!" she dared and folded her arms across her chest. Prince smiled and turned on her TV. Her eyes went wide at the reports of the vampire party. She blinked in disbelief when he stepped over to the window and in the direct sunlight.

"Take the cure. The government knows it works. They want me to kill a few stubborn vampires and then I'll take it, too," he assured her.

"Then I'll wait, too. Once you're done we can—" she protested but he cut her off. He could hear three heartbeats in the room and shared the news.

"You're pregnant. Take the cure before it harm's our baby," he said softly. Kristine paused to process his words. That would explain the missed period before she turned her self into a vampire. She had chalked it off as the stress of her life but this made more sense.

"Okay, I will but I need to do one thing as a vampire before I turn back," she said with a wicked grin.

The couple of vampires commenced to making love like only a couple of vampires could. It was an intense, almost violent at times, display of carnal lust at it's most primitive level. Prince thought about Katrina for the first time in a long time when Kristine rode him at superhuman speed like she used to do. He quickly shook her out of his mind and enjoyed his own woman. Hours had past before their love making session came to a mutually climatic end.

"Now that part I just might miss!" Kristine laughed as they cuddled. She was still all woman and could have cuddled for hours if not days. Luckily, Prince was there to remind her of the bigger picture.

"The baby," he said and she rolled out of bed. Their quickie in the shower took another hour and they finally got dressed again. Kristine slipped back into researcher mode and set up her computers and cameras to document the cure in action.

"Kristine Musa demonstrating D.P. 1029..." she began. Prince stifled a smile off camera, knowing the DP part was named after him. The 1029 represented the one thousandth and twenty-ninth version of her cure.

She drew blood to show the live virus in her system. She killed it in a test tube then injected it into her system. Her mind and soul were in harmony and the cure quickly cured her. The violent pangs she witnessed in Daniel, Butta, and other vampires over the years stemmed from them resisting.

From that same soul that commands evil and didn't want to give in to the self reproaching soul, that was the only way to pave the way for the soul to rest. Once it did, the cure could take root.

She tested her blood once more and proved that it worked. The patent would eventually net her a billion dollars even though she would have given it up for free.

*****

Prince kept his word after rounding the country, finding and killing vampires in hiding. He wrapped up shortly before the birth of his son and let Kristine inject him.

"Your soul has to be in peace," she reminded him. "If not, it will kill you!"

"It is. I'm ready," he said with a nervous swallow that made Kristine smile. Nervousness is a human trait, so that meant he was ready. She pushed the plunger of the syringe and let the liquid enter his system.

Prince smiled at the empty needle as she withdrew it from his arm. The smile tapered off as he began to have a visible reaction. Suddenly, his face changed as he began to age. The first five years added a little fullness to his face. The second speckled his goatee with four or five greys like his dad.

Kristine began to panic since she had seen this before. One version had seemingly cured a thousand year old vampire but then he aged a thousand years in two minutes. The man was reduced to dust right before her eyes. Just like what was happening now.

Prince grew even more handsome when ten more years perfected his face. Then the aging process came to an abrupt end. A forty-year-old version of the Dark Prince reached up and touched his face. He looked at his hands then over to his woman.

"Am I..." he asked tentatively. Kristine wouldn't risk a guess and quickly took some blood. Her usually rock solid hands shook like a fall leaf in an October breeze as she tested it for any trace of his the virus. She obviously wasn't content with the first results, so she drew more and tested it again. Prince was ready to accept his fate when she repeated the test a third time. All the results were the same, so she lifted her head and gave him the news.

"Cured. Cured, and cured!" she said triumphantly as she showed him all three results. "Oh Prince, you're cured!"

"Call me Martin then. No more Dark Prince," he said. The couple hugged, kissed and began their happily ever after.

*****

"Martin! You're too high! Come down!" Kristine worried as her precocious three-year old ascended to the top of the monkey bars. She and Martin married and moved to England for a quiet life out of the limelight.

Shortly afterwards, she gave birth to healthy son who was a perfect blend of several ethnicities. Just as God mixed the different types of earth in the creation of Adam, this child was part Haitian, part black, part East Indian and part Egyptian.

His mixed heritage resulted in a hue in his skin somewhere in the middle of his mother's and father's. His hair was thick like daddy's, yet curly like his mama's. The votes were in and the child was gorgeous.

"He is a boy," Martin reminded. He knew falling from the top of the monkey bars is a right of passage. Their son was all boy and had to take his lumps as all boys do.

"I'm okay! Watch this, mommy!" little Martin said and jumped before his parents could protest.

Mommy gasped and covered her eyes as her little boy came speeding towards the earth. Meanwhile, Martin Senior was trying to remember the route to the nearest emergency room. Both were relieved when he landed safely on the ground and threw his hands up victoriously.

"Good job, son," Martin cheered and clapped.

"Don't encourage him!" Kristine protested as the child suddenly snapped his head to the left as if someone called his name. A trickle of blood came out of one nostril and alerted his parents. She rushed to his side while he turned his head to see what he was looking at.

It turned out to be a who, not a what. Martin couldn't believe his eyes, so he blinked them rapidly and shook his head. It did nothing to clear his vision and Katrina Vladimir still approached. Her slinky, sultry walk had changed in centuries.

Martin wasn't totally shocked to know she was still alive because he didn't believe Butta possessed the powers to kill her. She was obviously even more powerful now since she walked freely during the midday sunrays. She too was now a day walker.

"There can be only one," Katrina said with an eerie smile.

"But we're mortal! My wife and I, we're human," Martin pleaded.

"Not you, or her," Katrina said and looked directly at their son. "Him. The boy."

Martin watched Katrina as she walked away, but he knew this wouldn't be the last time he would see her. She would be back for their special son one day, and they would be ready.

"Who was that?" Kristine asked since it was obvious by the awe on his face that she was somebody.

"Nobody. Let's go home," Martin said and took his family home.

The story is over but it's far from...

Chapter 21

"Well, hello there, handsome!" a lovely lady sang in that voice lovely ladies sing in when trying to get laid.

"Hello, yourself!" the handsome man sang back in a baritone voice of a dude with some dick to donate.

The bar was packed tonight, but they had made eye contact from across the room and mutually gravitated towards each and met in the middle. They were on the dance floor, so they danced. More like swayed to the jazz quartet on the stage.

"Would you like to go somewhere quiet?" she asked after a few minutes of verbal foreplay. She watched his movements enough to know he could move his hips like she liked.

"I would rather go somewhere loud and sweaty," he suggested instead. The slow smile that spread on her face spoke before her head began to nod and her mouth began to open.

"Loud and sweaty is just how I like it!" she said with a wicked smile.

"Mind if my wife joins us?" he asked which explained the pretty woman who came upon them.

"The more the merrier!" she agreed and off they went. The swinging couple took the woman to their hotel, which was fine by her. She knew how messy a threesome could be. "I'm going to devour you both!"

"We know," the wife said. They made a quick walk through the Toronto downtown district and went inside the swank hotel.

The couple usually went for C class motels to do their dirty work, but they were in a hurry. Life had just thrown a new curve that they needed to tend to. Business before pleasure even though their business was a pleasure.

"Mmmm, where do I start?" the woman asked as they entered the room. The married couple both stripped down to their skivvys and

141

were equally impressive. He was a chunk of deep chocolate while she was a creamy caramel delight.

"Let's start with some head," the wife said and whipped a solid silver sword from beneath the bed.

The guest went from shock to shocking in an instant. A loud hiss emitted as her fangs and claws popped out. Kristine took a swing that would have taken off her head, but the vampire sprang and gripped the ceiling above.

"Another one!" Martin announced and pulled the crossbow. Lately they had run across vampires who were stronger and harder to kill. He took aim and sent a couple stakes her way.

"Missed me, bitch!" she said as she scurried out of the way along the ceiling. Now it was her turn to attack. She was a blur of fangs and claws as she first went after Kristine.

Kristine managed to fight her off using the sword. Martin couldn't risk a shot since he might hit his wife. He played it safe and went for the tranquilizer gun. He fired at her back but she quickly spun and snatched the dart out of the air. She flung it and caused it to lodge in the ceiling. The distraction gave Kristine a shot and she took it.

"Ha-yah!" she grunted and took a swipe that took her leg off. That caused another distraction that gave Martin a chance to attack, as well. He swung his own sword and lopped off her arm.

"Ta-dah!" the woman vampire sang as the limbs hopped up on their own and reattached themselves.

"The fuck !" the couple said in unified amazement. The lady vampire lolled her head back in laughter, but she who laughs last often loses their head. The vampire hunting couple both swung their swords simultaneously. Martin's blade cut straight through her face and cut her head in half. Kristine's blade hit her throat and knocked her head completely off.

They both frantically chopped, sliced and dice the severed head into several pieces. Then, stomped the pieces as if doing the river dance. They were breathless and spent when they stepped back to watch and wait. To their relief, it did the trick and the vampire stayed dead. Kristine put a stake through the heart just in case.

Vampires were on the rise all over the world. They often battled each other to bloody conclusions unless the Jones got to them first. There was a worldwide battle for supremacy because there can only be one.

CHAPTER 22

Martin and Kristine sat and stared at the little boy watching TV in front of them. He had finally told her about Katrina and they both wondered if it were true. *Was their child a vampire?* they asked themselves now that they both watched him closely for signs of the supernatural.

"He can fly," Kristine said as proof of his paranormal prowess.

"He didn't fly. It was just a good jump," Martin said in defense of his jump from the top of the monkey bars.

"A good jump for an Olympian maybe," she shot back. Kristine closed her eyes and scrunched her face at the child's back.

"What are you doing?" her husband asked in a whisper.

"Seeing if he can read my thoughts!" she said as if he should have known.

"Well, that's just crazy, Kristine," Martin laughed heartily. A little too heartily and she snapped her head in his direction.

"Mmhm, you already did that, huh?" she nodded and he nodded along with her. They both knew what needed to be done but hadn't done it yet.

Kristine would have to draw his blood so it could be tested. However, she, like any other mother, didn't like to hurt her child and the child did not like needles.

"Can we see BimBo?" Martin junior pleaded and bounced up and down while pointing at the clown on the screen.

"What the heck is a BimBo?" his father wanted to know. Not that it really mattered since he gave his wife and child anything their hearts desired.

"BimBo is the one I was telling you about. He'll be in Manchester this weekend," Kristine replied.

"Oooh!" Martin nodded like he remembered, but he didn't remember.

"You don't remember," Kristine laughed since she knew her husband well. "Anyway, your son just loves him."

"So I guess we're going to Manchester," Martin sighed. His family was his world, so they could have and do whatever they wanted.

Little Martin played himself to sleep so his father picked him up and carted him up to his room. Kristine was wide awake, but he still carried her up the stairs, as well. She paid for the trip with kisses along the way, then gave him a tip when they reached their bedroom.

"Mmmm," Martin moaned when she planted a kiss on the tip, then a long lick on the shaft.

"Easy, buddy," she laughed when his knees buckled and helped him on the bed. He was mortal now, so she now had the advantage in the sack. He followed her lead which led to a screeching orgasm.

"My turn," Martin declared and took control. Come to find out, vampire or no vampire, he was still quite the dick slinger. The couple copulated for an hour until they were both breathless and satisfied. Then they cuddled up to chat until sleep came to claim them.

"Not bad for an old man," Kristine complimented. She always got a kick of reminding him that he was in his seventies. The cure settled him around forty years old that made them the same age.

"And you're not bad for a cougar," he quipped since she had been his senior. They bantered back and forth like couples deep in love tend to do. Finally, the mood darkened when they arrived back to the inevitable.

"We could just give him a dose of the cure. Why take chances? Katrina will come for him one day," she said with worry in her tone.

Martin and Kristine were the premier vampire hunters in the world. The outbreak of vampire attacks were steady on the rise, so they traveled the world subtracting them. Still, she was deathly afraid of Katrina. She was a daywalker and those are the most powerful ones. Martin was one himself until he let her cure him.

"And we'll be ready for her when she does!" he shot back immediately. It sounded good enough for a nuzzle from his wife even if he
wasn't quite so sure inside. "Besides, we can't give him the cure for a
few reasons."

"I'm listening," Kristine replied and leaned up. She was hoping to
he convinced so she could put those worries to bed.

"First, we don't even know if he has it. He's normal. He eats normal food, drinks juice boxes by the dozen. Plus, the kid loves the sun!
No way is he a vampire!" he said, sounding somewhat like a used car
salesman.

"And two?" she asked, hoping for more. He was right so far, but
that didn't explain why Katrina came to them.

"Two is the cure is determined by the will. There is no way we can
know what his will is. If he were a carrier, the cure could kill him," he
explained. That settled the matter once and for all since she would
not risk her child's life.

"I still need to draw his blood," she said and flipped over. He embraced her from behind so they could sleep. This also helped in the
morning since all she had to do was lift her leg and he would slide
right in.

*****

"Good to see the place has bounced back!" Kristine nodded approv-
ingly when they reached the city of Manchester, England. The city
was hit by some fool blowing himself up after a concert in the name
of Allah. She came from a Muslim family herself and knew enough
to know terrorism has nothing to do with Islam.

"Yeah," Martin agreed with mixed emotions in his tone as he
drove. Kristine turned her head to investigate until she saw what he
was looking at. Her head began to shake along with his when she saw
the group of teens dressed like vampires.

"Had it been dark, I would have hopped out and hit them with it!" she growled, then casted a glance into the backseat at their son. He was still singing the BimBo song along with his tablet.

The couple hunted vampires for a living as well as for the fun of it. The vampire craze led to some close calls and imitators almost getting a stake through their heart. The "it" Kristine spoke of was a semi-automatic crossbow that shot wooden stakes. It was just part of the bag of tricks they kept in their arsenal.

Silver bullets, silver chains, and silver infused tranquilizer darts also helped capture or kill. If worse came to worse, they kept and ace up their sleeves, locking it in a safe for safekeeping.

"Reminds me of the little black boys back home in America. They play dress up like thugs and goons and the white cops can't tell the difference," he sighed.

"Don't forget the little black girls doing the same," she reminded of the good girls dressing like thots. "For some reason, no one wants to dress up like Steve Jobs or Sir Richard Branson!"

They went back and forth about the perils of puberty until they arrived at the venue. BimBo was such a big draw, they had to rent an arena for several shows. Little Martin along with a million other kids fell in love with the charismatic clown. He had a hypnotic affect that affected the pockets of parents all over Europe.

Parents were strong-armed by whiny kids to buy BimBo shoes, BimBo dolls, BimBo lunch boxes, and everything else with his likeness. There were movies, slippers, games, and even juice boxes. Kids may have loved him, but some parents wished he was dead.

"BimBo, BimBo, BimBo," Little Martin cheered as they entered the venue. He joined the tens of thousands of other chanting children.

"Jim Jones," Kristine mumbled under her breath. They were seated in the expensive front row and watched the show.

Martin and his wife managed to get through the three-hour show then lined up so their son could take pictures with his favorite clown. Both wondered who was really behind the heavy makeup and red nose. She decided to find out once the show was over.

"Mommy will be right back," Kristine sang as she strapped her child into his seat.

"Okay, mommy," he happily agreed since daddy had far less rules. She grabbed a bag from the trunk and made her way back inside.

"Excuse me ma'am, you can't go in there!" a burly security guard said when she reached the clown's dressing room. She disagreed with a karate chop to his neck. He agreed with the blow and took an impromptu nap on the spot.

"Uh! Oh, it's not what it looks like!" BimBo blurted when Kristine barged in on him. He took his fangs out of the woman's neck and let her drop limply below.

"Well, that's good because it looks like you're a blood sucking vampire who leaves a trail of orphans after every show," she suggested even though she knew the answer.

The clown used his cover as an entertainer to stay under the radar. Being a vampire or vampire helper was all the rage, but the smart ones still tried to remain in the shadows. Theirs was a dynamic duo of vampire hunters leaving a trail of vampire ashes on every continent.

BimBo went on the attack when he realized who she was and why she was here. His fangs were already out as he leaped across the room in a blur. He may have been fast but she was faster.

Kristine whipped the crossbow out and let two stakes go. BimBo hissed as the wooden projectiles entered his body. He landed with a thud and she was on top of him. Two more stakes pinned him to the floor below.

"Now you can live or die. The choice is yours," she explained clearly as she pulled a syringe of cloudy liquid.

"No!" the clown hissed and roared as she jabbed the needle into his forehead. She pressed the plunger in and injected her cure or kill depending on his will.

Kristine took a step back since some vampires imploded when injected. They fight so hard, they just blow up and she had just washed her hair. No one wants vampire guts in their freshly washed hair.

BimBo shook and shivered as he fought the internal changes he was going through. Kristine just shook her head. It always amazed her how many vampires chose death over life. They resisted the cure and got the kill instead.

"Your choice," she told the dying vampire on her way out of the door. The guard was still napping as she stepped out of the dressing room. No sooner than the door closed, a loud pop echoed through the space. The insides of the clown were now on the outside of the clown. She gratefully patted her curls and hopped in the car with her favorite guys.

"When can we see BimBo again?" Little Martin wanted to know.

"If he comes back to town," she agreed, knowing he was now out of business.

CHAPTER 23

"But we love it here," Kristine whined as a last appeal. They had debated the pros and cons before she resorted to whining.

"And Katrina does, too," Martin reminded and sealed the deal.

"I guess America isn't too bad?" she asked since he was right. Katrina had popped up several times at several places. She never said a word when she appeared. Just stared at their child and licked her lips. Neither tried to kill her because she was too strong. If she killed them, no one could protect their child.

"Yes, America is bad. Still, which city shall we live in?" he answered and asked. They had enough money to live comfortably in any city of the country.

"Atlanta has bad memories," she suggested right off the bat to eliminate that option.

"California? Nah. New York!" Martin exclaimed. He watched his wife ponder for a few seconds before her head began to nod. New York was a big enough city to get lost in. Plus, there were frequent vampire reports in the tri-state area.

"It would cut down on travel expenses," she reasoned. With that, the Jones family was moving back to America.

Their English chateau was traded for a midtown high rise. Once they were settled in, they resumed their routine of taking their son to the park.

"He's going to have to lose the accent before school. These New York kids are rough," Martin teased of their prim and proper child.

"I suppose, 'yo son' and 'sup, B' would be more to your liking?" Kristine shot back. "Besides, he's a vampire. He can take care of himself."

"That boy is not a—" Martin was saying until their son made another huge leap off the swing. He still wasn't convinced but could only hope he wasn't.

"Father? Will you come swing with me?" the polite boy asked. His father hopped up immediately and went to play with his son. The proud mother watched her man and little man run, skip, hop and jump around the playground.

"Are you okay?" she asked when she noticed her husband winded and sweating after a few minutes of play. She knew how much stamina the man possessed since she put it to the test almost nightly.

"Huh? Yeah, I'm fine!" Martin said and stuck his chest out. He was the typical male and felt invincible. He had been nearly invincible for fifty years as a vampire, but he never felt more human than now.

"Okay, baby," she relented. The family went home, ate a family dinner, and fed their child desert. After a bath and bedtime story, it was time for adult desert. Martin read classic Aesop fables to the boy whether he understood it or not. They bonded over the stories before he drifted off to sleep.

"He's ummm," Martin announced as he entered the bedroom but his wife stole his train of thought. All she had on was a pair of riding boots and a smirk. "Going somewhere?"

"Yes sir!" Kristine laughed and pushed him on the bed. She could get aggressive at times and this was one of those times.

"Oh my," Martin joked when she roughly snatched his pants down

It obviously turned him on because his dick stood at full attention like a good soldier should.

"Oh my!" she repeated as she mounted him and worked him inside. Both mentally buckled up for the ride since she was in one of those moods.

Kristine began to wiggle and rock with her husband deep inside of her. She kept her eyes closed most of the time except to gauge the pleasure on his face. The way his face twisted and contorted, she knew he was enjoying it.

"Mmmm," Martin moaned and made his wife furrow her brow in confusion. She knew what it meant, but it was way too soon for that. She hoped she was wrong, but he went stiff and proved her right when he came with a shiver and a shudder.

"Noooo!" she moaned in sorrow. She still had a ways to go before she got there.

"My bad," he apologized sincerely and slightly embarrassed. Quick nuts can happen to the best of them from time to time and this was obviously one of those times.

"Awe, man," Kristine whined and rolled. She still had her boots on so she took matters into her own hands and finished herself off. Martin provided some support by sucking her nipples and caressing her body. Soon it was her turn to shiver and shudder.

"Long day," he apologized once again once she recovered and cuddled up next to him for sleep.

"It was," she agreed and planted a kiss on his lips. Then squinted and looked closer. "You have more wrinkles around your eyes."

"Do I?" he asked but didn't wait for an answer. He rolled out the bed and went into the bathroom to see for himself. He did see for himself as well as a few new greys in his temples. "Well, I am in my seventies."

"You are," she smiled softly at their running joke. Still she was concerned when she snuggled against his chiseled chest and went to sleep.

*****

Martin and Kristine awoke in the same position they went to sleep in. That made it easy to make love before the king in the next room awoke and stole the show. He rolled over on top of her and slid safely inside of her.

They traded kisses and moans as he humped them both to a mutual climax. They stole some more kisses and enjoyed the last of their alone time until naptime because their demanding child demanded attention.

"Mummy, father," came the call and knock on the door that signaled the Martin Jones Junior show.

"He will have to lose the mummy. The kids will think he's a sissy and pick on him," Kristine agreed to her husband before answering her son. "We'll be out in a few minutes."

"Okay, mummy," Little Martin sang and skipped away. Big Martin just shook his head.

"Baby!" Kristine shrieked when they made eye contact. The look of horror on her face sent him rushing into the bathroom. He expected some gross pimple in desperate need of popping but saw far worse.

"What the..." he marveled at the older man in the mirror. He reached out and touched the wrinkles on the mirror before touching the ones on his face.

"You're aging rapidly!" his wife said urgently when she rushed in behind him. They both looked at and touched the wrinkles and greys that had sprouted up over night.

Kristine turned him to face him and they had a tacit conversation as to what had to be done. They had spoken about this particular what if, on many of occasions but the occasion had arrived. The lasting effects of the cure were still unknown since he was her first success. There were plenty of cures after him, but he was the first. Now that the aging process had began, when would it stop? Would he keep advancing until his real age? Would he die of old age along the way?

Kristine wasn't down to find out. At the rate he had aged overnight, he would be an old man by lunch. She squinted to make her point and he nodded in agreement.

"Tuh!" she huffed to let him know she didn't need his approval. Then rushed off to retrieve one of the vials of blood she had drew before turning him back into a mortal. Martin was still squinted at the replica of the grandfather he lost long ago when she returned.

"If this doesn't work," he began but didn't get to the end of his sentence.

"This will work!" she insisted and she attached a needle to the vial, turning it into a syringe.

He blinked and watched as the tip entered his mortal skin. Watched as she drew up some of his mortal blood, before depressing the plunger and injecting him with his immortal blood.

"I love you and Martin," he groaned as a sharp pain wracked him in half.

"We love you, too. Now, go ahead and die so you can come back to us," she said as he curled into a fetal position on the floor. Kristine showered and stepped over her dead husband to fix breakfast for her son.

"Mummy, where is father?" Little Martin asked, looking down the hall for the man.

"He's not feeling well. And for now on, call me ma. Call your father pops. You got it!" she barked with the frustration of the day evident in her voice.

"Okay, ma," he said like a real New Yorker. He still had a ways to go, but so did his pops.

*****

"Well, look who's up!" Kristine cheered when her dead husband stirred back to life. It took longer than she expected and two days had passed by with a corpse in the corner.

"Am I?" he asked and felt himself up. First he made sure he was alive since he remembered being dead. He felt his conflicted soul bouncing around inside of his frame. Angels from both heaven and hell came to claim him but it wasn't his time. Not just yet.

"Well, you're alive," she said for sure since she had checked for a pulse while he was dead and didn't find one. "How do you feel?"

"Thirsty. How do I look?" he asked and touched his face, then teeth. Last he reached down and gripped his dick.

"You look good!" Kristine cheered. Martin took off into the bathroom to get a look for himself.

"I do look good," he said and admired his old/new self in the mirror. He had aged close to sixty by the time Kristine injected him, but had reversed to his mid thirties. He made a grimace to see his fangs and they slowly slid back out. The Dark Prince was back.

"Here you go," his darling wife said and handed him a pack of plasma when he returned.

"Thanks," he thanked and sank his fangs inside. She produced another as he drained the first. He felt stronger with every drop but still didn't know which of his powers remained.

"I'm sure glad it worked," she said with a sigh. Prince read between the lines, then peered inside her head and read her mind.

"No, baby!" he moaned, even though it was too late to stop it. The deed was done and Kristine had injected herself with his blood, as well.

"I won't live without you," she explained and began the process of dying. "Tell Martin I'll see him in a couple of days."

"See you soon," he said and kissed her forehead. Prince tucked his wife in bed so she could die in peace.

CHAPTER 24

"Will Mrs. Jones be returning tonight?" Abbey asked when Prince emerged from his bedroom. He called the babysitter over so he could spread his wings a little until his wife awoke from her slumber.

"Perhaps," he said and ignored her batting eyes and big breast. He wasn't sure why his wife selected the flirty white girl from the agency but wished she would wake up to deal with her.

"Mom's coming back tomorrow," young Martin proclaimed since he told him two days. He planned to hold his father to it just like he held his mother to when Prince died for a couple days.

"Mom is coming back tomorrow," he agreed and kissed his son's forehead. The babysitter looked up like she wanted one too but he turned to leave.

"One more movie and it's bedtime," Abbey sang as she watched the boy's handsome father exit the apartment. With Mrs. Jones away, she wanted to make sure the child was sleep when Mr. Jones returned. This way she could have him all to herself.

Meanwhile, Prince needed to get out into the night and spread his wings. That's if he still had wings. He still had no idea what powers he had retained other than reading minds. The sloppy blowjob the babysitter pondered on gave him a good laugh even though he wouldn't take her up on it. He had long ago read the police report of his own father's death and infidelity would be a problem he and his wife would never have. He just hoped she awoke soon since she could give a pretty sloppy blow job herself when she wanted to.

Prince was a daywalker before the cure but didn't risk the sunlight just yet. He decided to take baby steps to see which of his powers remained. A flamboyant vampire up in the Bronx was making a lot of noise and getting a lot of attention. He had made it on their list anyway but once the man started turning children, he couldn't wait for Kristine to wake up.

156

Mario had been a low level mafioso type up in the Bronx borough. He was regulated to being a driver and do-boy until he ventured into a vampire party one night. The parties moved from city to city every since someone turned into a wolf and ate a bunch of them in Atlanta. Then he had his manager, Meech, blow the roof, and burn the rest in the sun.

"Did I do that?" Prince laughed at the memory as he ran swiftly along the highway towards the Bronx.

Mario had began turning children to start his own army after killing all the other mafia men in the neighborhood. Now he had the power to rule the borough. He fed indiscriminately and left the street littered with corpses. The city filed a complaint and got him put on the vampire hunter's hit list. It was more of a shit list since that's what they turned them into.

Prince took a deep breath and made a huge leap when he reached the Hudson River. He couldn't quite fly again just yet but easily cleared the body of murky brown water filled with bodies and other assorted debris. He mentally mashed the gas and covered several blocks with each step. A few minutes after leaving his apartment, he arrived on Mario's block.

"Hey, mister. Want a date?" a little girl asked when Prince reached the block.

"Sure," he agreed since he read her mind and knew what she really wanted to give him in the alley. He could feel the gathering of vampires lurking in the dark alley. He still followed her as did many men looking for desert only to become dinner.

This was how Mario's street urchins fed at night, while Mario preyed on mothers, fathers, and children. Not only does the heart survive when one is turned, it is enhanced. Whatever was in it before will be dialed up to the max. The good heart will still contain good despite having to feed for survival. That's why Claude opened the blood bank and Daryl fed on street criminals. The bad hearts became even more corrupt and inflicted as much damage as it could muster.

Prince's heart contained a mix of good and bad. Mirth and malice, as well as forgiveness and vengeance. The mix made him compassionate and dangerous. These kids were about to get either side and didn't even know it.

"Ahhh!" the child screamed and attacked. Prince let her jump on him and bite into his neck, as ten more vampire children popped out of their hiding places. The girl got a taste of his blood and hopped off just as quickly. "What are you?"

"I'm what you're not," he replied and whipped out one of the few weapons he brought along with him. He and Kristine used to pack a bag full of vampire killings weapons when they were mortals. Now that he was turned, he was a vampire-killing weapon himself.

The kids laughed when they saw the funny looking gun he produced. They all had been shot at least once since they began attacking humans. This was the Bronx after all and everyone was strapped.

"Don't fight it," he warned and took aim. The children laughed when the darts lodged into their bodies. It was real funny until the cure began to spread through their bodies.

Some took heed to his warning and let the magic happen. Some others enjoyed the chaos they could cause as vampires and resisted. As a result, some died while others lived and Prince was okay with that.

"Now for Super Mario!" Prince growled and turned. He left the dead and dying kids behind. He followed the scent of the vampire up into a walkup building and knocked on the door with his foot.

"What the fu—" Mario began to ask of the sudden intrusion. He was busy sucking blood from one woman while another sucked him below the waist at the same time.

The fuck of his "what the fuck" got caught in his throat when Prince clamped his teeth into his neck. He could have quickly drained him dry but chose to snatch his throat away instead. Both woman had fresh bite marks in their necks and stuck their faces in the fountain spewing from his neck.

"Ummm, not," Prince declined and used one swipe of his claws to remove both of their heads. "There can be only one and y'all ain't it!"

*****

Prince used to have to clean up behind himself when he made a massacre. Now he left a mess as a deterrent to other vampires. It worked about as much as states enacting the death penalty. Gangs still banged and thugs kept right on thugging. People kept wanting to get turned, so he would keep on turning them back into mortals or turning them into corpses. The choice was theirs.

Prince felt a surge of power after killing Mario but still didn't have wings. He would take it slow and build his strength. When Katrina came for his son, he would be ready.

Meanwhile, Abbey had just tucked little Martin in his bed and plotted on how to get Mr. Jones in bed next. She stripped naked and stretched out on the sofa so her plump, freshly shaved box would be the first thing he saw when he stepped in. She was so worked up she reached down and rubbed one out to take the edge off.

"Even better!" she cheered at her next bright idea. Why not be face down, ass up in his bed since his wife was out of town she thought? Her head nodded with her bright idea while she went towards his room.

The door was locked but that never stopped her before. She rushed into the kitchen and retrieved the universal master key, otherwise known as a butter knife. She jimmied the lock and shimmied inside.

"Hmph," she said to herself of the lump under the comforter. She planned to fuck Mr. Jones in that same spot, so it would have to go. A loud screech filled the night air when she pulled the cover away and saw the corpse.

"Uh oh," Prince said when he arrived at his building. The heavy police presence had him on high alert. He could only hope what ever happened didn't happen to his family. That hope was dashed when he arrived up to his floor and saw his door open.

"There he is!" Abbey proclaimed and pointed at Prince as he walked into his door.

"What's the problem here?" he asked, then squinted when he saw his door ajar. He was poised to pounce and slaughter them all if need be. If it came to that, he would claim they were all vampires who came to kill him before he could kill them. He remained calm when he realized they just arrived.

"We got a call of a dead body?" the cop asked Prince, then looked at the caller.

"His wife! In there!" Abbey shouted and pointed at the bedroom door. She left out the how she got in along with the why.

"My wife? She—" Prince was saying before being interrupted.

"Is trying to sleep! I'm dead tired," Kristine said with a yawn and stretch as she stepped out.

"But she was, I saw her, I—" Abbey protested like she was upset to see the woman alive. Prince peered into her head and stifled a laugh. She was still thinking about getting laid.

"Sorry to bother you guys," the cop said and turned to leave. There was an awkward moment of silence as Abbey searched for her next words.

"Sorry?" Prince suggested without forcing it on her.

"Yeah!" the airhead cheered and repeated. "I'm sorry I was going to and then she, and we—"

"You can leave now," Kristine added. Abbey nodded and quickly gathered her things. She cast a last glance at Prince's crotch like the one that got away and scurried along her way.

"How you feel, babes?" Prince asked and rushed to her side.

"Thirsty!" she declared and looked to the door Abbey just left.

"I figured you would be," Prince said and rushed to retrieve a pack of plasma. His wife was in the mirror looking at herself when he returned.

"My smile lines are gone! And look at my boobies!" she happily admired. Kristine had shed a few middle-aged mommy pounds. Her boobs were bigger and firmer, plus her stomach was chiseled. His eyes went wide at the sight of her six-pack. Her eyes went wide at the sight of the blood.

"Guess I'll grab another," he suggested as she greedily sucked down he first pack. He returned with the other and she slurped it down, as well.

"Are you thinking what I'm thinking?" she asked and ran her tongue over her fangs.

Prince passed on going inside her mind to see. Not that he had to since it was written all over her face. He scooped her up by her firmer ass and slid his tongue in her mouth. She reached down and guided him inside of her. It was off to the races until the sun peeked over the horizon. They could have gone all day but knew their child would come knocking soon.

Kristine was first to blow but her husband was right behind her. They showered, and dressed to start a new day in their new lives as immortals.

CHAPTER 25

"What are you doing?" Kristine asked when Prince walked over to the window and reached for the curtain. The blackout drapes protected the vampires from the deadly sun.

"I was a daywalker once. Perhaps I am once again," he said and pulled the drapes open. Kristine scrambled out of the way so none of the rays reached her.

Prince put his hands on his hips, defiantly and looked up into the rising sun. It looked good for a few seconds until he started to smoke and sizzle. He tried to grin and bare it but it got the best of him.

"Shit!" he cursed and fell away. He pulled the cord and shut the dangerous rays out where they couldn't hurt him.

"Smells like bacon," Kristine laughed at her smoking husband.

"Ha, ha," he laughed dryly. "We need strength. Vampires are evolving!"

"He what?" she shrieked when Prince recounted the events of the night before. She rushed over to her computer to add this new development to her notes.

Vampires regenerating was a new phenomenon around the globe. Now they were regrowing limbs as if they weren't hard enough to kill as it were.

"We have to get stronger!" Prince repeated. They needed to find and kill as many vampires as they could, as fast as they could.

"Looks like we'll get our chance!" she cheered and turned the screen towards him. Both bared their fangs as they read about another vampire jamboree coming soon.

"A-yo, ma? Pops!" young Martin called as he knocked on the door. His parents retracted their fangs before inviting him in.

"Hello, son," she sang as the boy came into the room and hopped on the bed.

"Can we go to the park today?" he asked like he always did. The family had always gone as a family but lately only one parent had been taking him since the other one had been busy dying.

"Um, we, she, and I have," Kristine stammered and looked to her husband for help.

"I'll call Abbey," he said. It was already out of his mouth before he thought about it, so he shrugged and made the call. Kristine ignored her babbling boy in favor of listening to her husband. She wanted to hear how he planned to work this out.

"Hello?" Abbey asked as she tentatively took the call. She wanted to crawl under a rock after the embarrassing episode.

"Hey, Abbey. We were wondering if you could take Martin to the park? The wife and I both have a ton of work," he explained.

"Me? After ummm, sure. Okay!" she decided since she did need the money. If the couple wanted to act like nothing happened, then she would too. "I'm on my way!"

"She's on her way," Prince relayed as he hung up.

"Yes, please," Martin Junior nodded to his mother.

"Yes, what?" she asked of the answer without a question.

"You just asked if I wanted a sandwich. Yes," he said and scrunched his face like she was tripping. He reached his backhand to her forehead to see if she had a fever.

"I didn't say anything?" she said to her son, then her husband. "Did I?"

"You must have," Prince insisted since he knew what it meant if she didn't. Kristine deliberately pressed her lips together and looked at little Martin. Prince held his breath, hoped for the best, and got the worse.

"Yes, mommy. Okay, mommy," the little one said in response to questions his mother merely thought about. He hopped up and went to get dressed and left his shocked parents to deal with it.

"That doesn't necessarily mean, I mean... he eats food. Loves the sun," Prince offered as his wife nodded eagerly for an explanation. Any explanation other than their child being a vampire.

"He may just have strong intuition. I tell him to get dressed every day. He wants waffles every day, too!" Kristine added. She knew she wouldn't find out until she took his blood. Even that was no guarantee that she could determine what was up with her son.

"Yeah," Prince sighed and changed the subject by turning on the TV. The news report of a vampire attack in nearby Queens bought smiles to both of their fangs. They needed to catch and kill as many vampires as possible as much as possible.

"The door!" their child yelled over the melodic chimes of the doorbell. Kristine was married to a man, so she didn't budge. Meanwhile, Prince stood and went to answer.

"Hello, Mr. Jones," Abbey greeted shyly and ducked her head. It was a genuine display but she still peeked at his crotch.

"Good morning, Abbey. Come in," he said and stepped aside. He shook his head at the thoughts booming out of her head as she walked in.

"Hello, Martin! Mrs. Jones," she greeted to the other occupants.

"You guys have fun. We've had a long night, so we're going to take a nap," Kristine told the babysitter and her son and took her husband by the hand.

"See you guys later!" Abbey sang and waved. She shot one more glance at Prince's crotch and thought about what she would do with it.

"Well, at least we won't have to tell him about the birds and the bees," Prince chuckled and followed his wife to bed.

*****

"We're going to be the biggest gang in this borough. This city, state, and country!" Shark told his gang. His crooked teeth earned him the nickname, Shark, when he was young, but now they came in handy after being turned at a vampire party

"Yeah!" his gang of newly made vampires cheered back. None of them yet possessed the power to read minds and had no idea what was really on his mind.

Shark had accidentally killed a vampire and felt the rush of power that came with it. The next two kills were no accidents. Nor would the fifty new recruits standing in front of him.

"We..." he said, then stopped dead in his tracks. His head snapped up towards the strong presence he felt above. All heads followed and looked at the large bat hovering above while Kristine walked into the front door.

"Knock, knock," she sang and knocked the heads off of two vampires with her silver sword.

Most times, they brought along the cure to give vampires a chance to turn back. This wasn't most times and all of these vampires were dying tonight. The bat transformed into a man and floated to the floor.

"The Dark Prince," Shark snarled and bared his claws. He had been talking a lot of shit about what he would do if he ever came for him. So much shit, he actually started to believe it.

Kristine guarded the door with her sword while the vampires circled to watch the showdown. Shark's crew expected an epic battle, but they weren't going to get one.

"Hello, Shark," Prince growled. He flexed his powers and morphed into his wolf like creature. He lunged forward and bit Sharks head completely off. He spit it out and transformed back just as quickly. "Goodbye Shark."

The gang was relieved to see the wolf was gone, but it was short lived. Prince took a seat and let his wife attack the rest. Kristine chopped the vampires into bite-sized pieces. The ones who ran were gunned down with her crossbow. A few more were dispatched with bites that took chunks and plugs out of her victims. She felt a surge of energy flow into her body and being with each kill. Soon there were just a couple surrounded by empty shells.

"I feel..." Kristine said and paused to find the right words.

"Exuberance?" Prince offered.

"That too, but..." she squinted as the feeling came into view. A fanged smile spread across her bloody mouth when she figured it out. "Horny!"

"Ah yes!" Prince agreed since he often felt it too after a massacre. The blood and gore was the perfect backdrop for the impromptu love making session. Only the approaching dawn cut it short.

"Race you home?" Kristine challenged as they stepped back out into the crisp night air.

"You don't—" Prince began but found himself alone as he wife took flight. Literally since she could now fly, too. "Stand a chance" he finished.

Prince took a giant leap and spread his wings, as well. He quickly caught up to his wife and flew along side of her. He could easily have beat her, but what fun is that. They arrived back to their high rise and landed on the roof. After a few flights of stairs, they entered their apartment.

"Hello, Mrs. Jones. Mr. Jones," Abbey greeted groggily as they walked in.

"Abbey!" Kristine shrieked when the woman's indecent thoughts floated across the room. She frowned her face and rushed her husband into the bedroom.

"What?" Prince asked but his chuckle said he already knew.

"We need a new baby sitter!" she demanded. They slid into the shower and picked up where they left off earlier.

*****

"Next!" Kristine shouted and dismissed the next prospective babysitter. The agency sent their whole roster to fill the position. Kristine just knew this last prim and proper spinster was perfect until she read her mind.

"What was wrong with her?" Prince asked since he refused to look into their thoughts. He'd been a vampire long enough to know it's better not to know what people are thinking.

"She was high as a kite!" Kristine shrieked. Almost half were high off something, some wanted to steal and quite a few had impure thoughts about her husband as well as her.

"Well, that's all of them. What are we going to do now?" he wanted to know. They had plenty of vampires to kill and needed someone to watch their son while they did. They certainly couldn't drag him from city to city, state to state and country to country to kill vampires. Not to mention the park since neither could venture out during the day.

"There's one more. A student. She is scheduled for later tonight," Kristine said and stood. She was still a wife and mom, so she headed into the kitchen to cook dinner for her men. Meanwhile, little Martin bounced in to chat with his father.

"Out loud," Prince insisted when the child tried to send him his thoughts. The father sounded like an immigrant father demanding his children speak English in their new land.

"Sorry, dad," he said with a slight curtsey, reminding Prince that they had too many cable channels.

"No problem. What's up?" he asked. The doting dad and darling dude chatted it up until dinner. The family sat around the table and all ate together.

Martin was a throwback, old school family man since he was technically from another time. There were no cell phones or social media at the table. No TV or music to compete with pleasant conversation floating around the table. The parents needed to enjoy it while they could since their child would one day become a teenager. A teenage vampire at that.

"Huh?" Prince asked when he felt his senses tingle. It was the sense and scent of a vampire in the area.

"Go to your room!" Kristine told her son when she got a whiff a few seconds later. She escorted her son to his room and bared her fangs and guarded the door. Martin bared his as well as his fangs when a vampire knocked on the door.

CHAPTER 26

"Come in!" Prince growled and was poised to pounce. He was ready to transform into the wolf if Katrina walked into the apartment. Kristine too had a sword in one hand and the wooden stake, shooting crossbow in the other. The doorknob slowly turned and a woman poked her head in.

"Bad time?" the young vampire asked when she saw the two vampires in full battle mode.

"Melcina. The agency sent me," she said and they both relaxed. Kristine peered into her mind and smiled.

"Come on in!" she said and put her weapons away. They all sat around the large coffee table and conversed. They sipped packs of plasma instead of decaf as they interviewed her. She had all the qualifications and wasn't high. Kristine was also pleased to read no impure thoughts about her husband.

"So," Prince said and got down to the obvious question. "Who turned you?"

"My ex. I guess I'm lucky since he gave most of his other girlfriends herpes," she said with a shrug. "I'm from Cali originally. I came here for school."

Kristine nodded along with her story since she found no contradictory thoughts in her mind.

"So, where is this ex now?" Prince wanted to know. He was especially dangerous if he was passing out herpes and the vampire virus. Melcina gave up his whereabouts with a soft smile that contained the knowledge that she would never have to deal with him again.

"Well, Melcina, you can start this weekend," Kristine said and called little Martin out to seal the deal. Both parents smiled on as the newest addition to their family bonded with their boy.

"Do you think we should give her the cure?" Kristine asked once they were alone in bed.

"Yes. Just not yet," he said and explained why. "I'd rather have a vampire watching our child until we can kill Katrina."

"You mean if," his wife sighed. The room went silent as they pondered their future. It would be a short future if they didn't figure out a way to defeat the daywalker.

******

"Just let me put the tip in?" A.J pleaded desperately. He used the same line since he was a teenager, but now it had a different meaning. Now he was trying to stick the tip of his fangs into her femoral artery.

"It's gonna hurt," the young girl giggled as young girls had since he was a teen.

A.J hunted the virgins since their pure blood was untainted and delicious. Sweeter than the cherries he popped after he drank. He turned them out, then turned them like he did Melcina. She was the one who got away when she went out east to go to college. Prince had business out in Cali but made a detour to pay him a visit.

"No, it won't," A.J lied and took a long lick up her thigh, across her labia and down the other thigh.

"Yes, it will," Prince said as he swooped into the room. He winced from the high-pitched scream that accompanied his sudden appearance. "Now, A.J!"

"My bad. You scared me," the vampire said and tried to save face in front of his guest.

"You should be scared," Prince warned and inspected the girl. She was still mortal, so he quickly dismissed her with a, "Beat it!"

"Yes sir!" she blurted and gathered her clothes. Prince was very happily married but still stole a glance at her jiggling lady parts as she escaped.

"I know you! The Dark Prince! Man, I loved your music!" A.J gushed. He also knew of his new career as a vampire killer and hoped to flatter him into a pass. It may have worked if not for the fact that there can only be one.

"I need a list of names. Every girl you turned," he demanded. A.J made a sudden moved that almost cost him his life but only came up with his phone.

"Here," he said and passed it off. Prince just shook his head at the massive list of young women he had to turn back. "So, we good?"

"If, 'we' were French. We not though," Prince remarked. A.J still had a confused frown on his face as his head tumbled in mid air. One swift swipe from Prince's claws detached his head from his shoulders and soul from his body.

The rest of his California trip was spent tracking down and injecting new vampires with the cure. It only cure half since half wanted to remain vampires. Half of them died from the cure while Prince killed the others. Once he finished, it was time to head back to his family in New York.

*****

Meanwhile, Kristine was dealing with a dilemma of her own. The new vampire had plenty of plasma to sustain life but the urge to feed was getting stronger. Not to mention the taste of the pure blood straight from the source beckoned.

"I'm stepping out for a moment," she decided when the urge became to much to bear. Melcina saw the thirst on her face and knew exactly why she was stepping out.

"Have fun," the babysitter said. She was almost family now and spent time with Martin even when his parents were home. A day shift nanny took the boy to the park.

"Oh, I plan to," she said and eased out of the unit. Kristine was dressed to impress when she stepped out into the crisp New York night air. She looked both ways before deciding to hit the lower east side of Manhattan.

The section had a booming nightlife and was bustling with activity. The long line in front of a nightclub beckoned and she went over to investigate. A burly bouncer stuck his arm out to impede her from walking straight inside.

"Hundred bucks for VIP," he advised. She had saw him lifting the velvet rope for a select few while most waited in the line stretching down the block.

"Free for me," she corrected and his big head nodded instantly.

"Free for you," he repeated. Kristine stifled a giggle as she tried her powers of suggestion for the first time on someone other than her husband. She wasn't sure if it worked since Prince went down on her regularly anyway.

"Oh my!" Kristine swooned when she stepped inside. The sound of a thousand heartbeats boomed over the thunderous bass coming from the sound system. She swallowed hard and fought her fangs from coming out on their own.

She scanned through the darkness looking for a meal. Her heightened senses slowed the present down like a rap video. Booties and breast shook and bounced in slow motion all around. She searched for her dinner like a housewife selecting fruit in the market. A look over to the bad and she clearly saw a man lace a girl's drink while she turned her head. His friend distracted her by groping her booty.

"Yeah right," Kristine fussed of her playful protest. She picked up the drink and tossed it back before she could stop her. It was fine since she had found her dinner. It looked like it was going to be a two-piece meal when the men each took an arm to guide their prey from the club.

"You guys taking me home? To my home?" she naively asked as they escorted her out.

After we run a train on you and post the pictures and videos all over the internet, one thought. Kristine read both of their thoughts and found they were on the same page. Now they could be on the same plate, as well.

Kristine ran briskly along side the car like a black blur all the way it to Central Park, AKA the train station since many a train had been ran in the huge park.

"Here's good," one of the men suggested after looking around. Cheapskates were scattered all over with their cheap dates. The coast was clear and this was the perfect spot for a sexual assault.

"Good for what?" the woman slurred as they laid her down. The men had just began to remove her clothing when Kristine swooped in.

"There's a good spot!" she said and tossed one of the men up into the tree above.

"What the—" the other began but didn't finish. He had bigger concerns to be concerned about when the vampire sank her fangs into his neck. Kristine went into a frenzy when she got that first gush of hot blood fresh from his heart. It wasn't moving fast enough for her, so she bit half of his neck away and slurped the gusher. She pulled his head back way further than God designed,with a sickening crunch of bone and cartilage.

"Oh wow!" she drunk woman said and squinted at the man's head lying almost on his back. Only the spine and shards of skin kept it from falling off and rolling away.

"I'm out of here!" his buddy decided from up in the tree. He wanted no parts of what was going on down below, so he made a break for it. Literally since his leg snapped loudly when he jumped out the tree.

"Oh, you're out of here alright!" Kristine agreed with a growl and attacked him too. The would be rapist woke up all the parks pigeons, squirrels and rats when he let out a blood curdling scream when he saw the large fangs coming towards him. Two cops were parked a block over and heard it in their cop car.

"Did you hear that?" one asked the other haltingly. The scream sent such a chill up his spine and he actually shivered.

"Nah, I didn't hear anything," his partner said after a shiver of his own. He turned up the window to make sure he couldn't hear what he didn't just hear again. The city didn't pay enough to tangle with the new threat of the vampires.

Kristine killed all screams and protests when she chomped into his throat. A larynx is needed for sound as she had just swallowed his. Animalistic sounds and snarls emitted from Kristine as she fed. Plasma and blood products weren't a match for fresh blood from a live victim as she drank every drop. The man's internal organs collapsed from the strong suction.

"Are you you going to kill me, too?" the suddenly sober woman stuttered.

"Nah, you're killing your self. Go home," Kristine said over her shoulder and did the same. She felt refreshed from the meal and knew plasma would never satisfy her again. She was now one of the monsters she hunted her whole life.

CHAPTER 27

"Hey, baby! How was your trip?" Kristine gushed when her husband returned from his trip out west. He didn't get to respond quickly enough and she rushed over and shoved her tongue into his mouth. She leapt into the air and wrapped her legs around his back.

"Great actually," Prince replied when she finally got off of him. He opened his mouth to tell her about the trip then stopped short when he noticed the changes in her.

"What?" she asked of his squinting as he gave her a once over.

"What is what did you do?" he asked and twisted his lips at the bull she started to come with. She let out a deep sigh, lowered her head and came clean.

"It's so good, baby! So fresh! So clean!" Kristine sang and actually did a twirl.

"It is, but we don't want to become part of the problem we're supposed to fix," he reminded.

"I know, I know but they really deserved it! There are plenty of bad people in this city. In every city. It's like killing two birds with one stone."

"Or two fangs," Prince added and came on board. Now not only were New York's vampire population in trouble, so was it's bad guys. He pulled himself away and went to his son's room for a peek. It was too late to play but after a week away, he wanted to at least look at the boy.

"Daddy! I mean sup, pops," young Martin greeted when Prince stuck his head in the room to check on him.

"Sup, buddy. Why aren't you asleep?" he asked as he came over and took a seat on his bed.

"I was until I felt you come in. It was loud," the child said and stole a hug.

175

"Heard me come in?" Prince asked since he was pretty sure he was pretty quiet. Especially since he had extra insulation put in his son's room since he and his wife could get pretty loud when they made love which was pretty often.

"I felt you. I always feel you and mommy. And Melcina. And the lady in the park," he said.

"What lady in the park?" Prince asked and felt light headed at the thought. He knew Katrina would find them. Just didn't think it would be so soon. They weren't ready to face her yet. "A white lady?"

"A Chinese lady. She sells hot dogs," he said and Prince frowned curiously. It was too late to do anything about it now, so he kissed his child on the forehead and tucked him back in. He wasn't sure how, but he had a date in the park tomorrow.

*****

"I feel like a real clown!" Prince protested after he got dressed.

"You look like a clown," Kristine seconded when she looked him up and down. He should look like a clown since he had on a full clown costume complete with the baggy clothes, big shoes, wig, and, more importantly, a full face of makeup that would allow him to travel by day.

"You sure you don't want to come with?" he asked hoping to get her in a clown costume as well. Then he could laugh at her just like she was laughing at him.

"I'll pass on this one. Just make sure to get her blood. At least a vial," she reminded.

"I'll get it all if she is a vampire!" he growled. They both wondered if vampires hadn't somehow morphed again. First, there was BimBo who neither could sense. Then, vampires growing back body parts. And now a possible daywalker in the same park their child played in.

"Either way," Kristine shrugged since she intended to rid the planet of each and every vampire. They say there can be only one, but that was one too many as far as she was concerned.

"That must be Evelyn," she added to the chimes ringing throughout the house.

"I'm not getting it," Prince fussed since he was in full clown regalia. Kristine cracked up again as she went to let the new nanny in. She was taking Martin to the museum today. Just in case the park became a crime scene.

"Good morning, Mrs. Jones. Is Martin ready?" the sweet lady sang as Kristine let her in.

"Good morning. He sure is," she replied and turned. "Martin!"

"Sup, ma," the little boy said sounding a little more like a New Yorker by the day.

"Miss Evelyn is here to take you to the museum today!" she informed. There was a tense silence as the boy peered into the woman's head. He found no malice and began to nod.

"Okay, ma," he agreed and grabbed his electronic devices for the road. Kristine called down to the driver so he could be ready. Prince came out the second they cleared the apartment.

"A'ight, ma. I'm out," Prince mocked and got mushed.

"You're the one who wanted him to lose his British accent!" she reminded. The child had been born in America but spent his first years of life in England. As a result, he sounded like the king of England. His father was right the rough New York kids would eat him alive if he went to school talking like that.

"I did," he agreed. She leaned in for a kiss, but Prince pulled back. "Don't mess up my makeup!"

"Never say that to me again, please," Kristine laughed. She blew him an air kiss as he stepped out. Prince took the stairs in a blur and stepped out into the sun light.

"Here we go," he said as he felt the sun for the first time since being turned back. He paused for the sizzle and burn but none came. The clown smile painted on masked the real smile underneath as he pranced over to the park.

"Hot dog! Aningkasao!" the Chinese lady sang in Korean since she actually was Korean. She was smiling, singing, and slinging hot dogs until she felt Prince enter the park. She was weary at first until she saw he was heading directly towards her.

"Shit!" Prince fussed when the woman took off at an incredible speed. He took a deep breath and took off after her. It looked like a real life cartoon of a cat chasing a mouse as they dipped, dodged, and leapt over benches. Except it was a clown chasing an elderly Korean, Chinese lady which was actually funnier.

"Ahhh!" the woman screamed when Prince caught up and pounced on her.

"Who are you! What are you!" he demanded when he pinned her to the ground. She rattled back in rapid fire Korean, but Prince didn't speak that. The best he could do was pull his phone and record her. Then he pulled the syringe and filled it with her blood.

"Ahhh!" she repeated and dropped dead. Prince stood and glanced around at all the spectators staring at the spectacle. He took a deep breath and turned into a colorful blur as he took off once again.

"How'd it go? Did you see her? Did you get it?" Kristine demanded as soon as Prince stepped back into the apartment.

"What's my name?" he asked and cocked his head like a boss. "Of course, I got it. Piece of cake!"

Kristine snatched the vial of blood and rushed into the spare bedroom that doubled as her lab. Most of the test would take days, but the process was started immediately.

*****

"Whew!" Prince cheered as their early morning sexual session came to a mutually climatic ending. Kristine panted and tried to catch her breath. They cuddled up and hit the TV remote to see what was happening in the city.

"A bizarre scene unfolded in Central Park yesterday..." the reporter reported.

"Uh oh," Prince said and went for the remote to change the channel. Not that it would have helped since it was on every station.

"Piece of cake, huh?" Kristine said as the footage of a clown chasing an old lady played on the TV. She could only shake her head as the woman scrambled up trees and over benches with her husband in hot pursuit.

"Nimble old broad," Prince mumbled when the old lady pulled an NFL worthy juke move and made him miss.

Kristine just shook her head and rolled off the bed. She put a little jiggle in her walk since she had an audience as she stepped into the bathroom to shower. It was no surprise when Prince came in behind her. The shower took a little longer since they ended up making love under both showerheads.

"Well, Mr. Clown. I have work to do," she said and wrapped herself in her plush robe instead of putting on clothes, so she could get to her lab that much sooner. The woman scientist was a certified lab rat and could spend days in there if left alone. No food or sleep, just numbers and formulas.

"Let's see what we have!" Kristine cheered and rubbed her hands together when she saw a message from Seoul South Korea. She had sent the video Prince took while he had the woman pinned to a colleague on the peninsula. Kristine skipped the message, ignored the time difference and made the cross continental call.

"Hello, Kim. What you got for me?" she asked when the call was answered.

"Let me start with the video of the clown chasing the woman! Oh my God. That was so funny!" she howled with laughter. Kristine tried not to laugh since the clown was her husband. Tried but failed and the two old friends yucked it up for a few minutes.

"Can we get to the translation, please?" Kristine asked after several minutes had past.

"Oh my god, you know him don't you! Was that?" she paused and looked. "It is! That's Martin!" Kim exclaimed and set off another round of uproarious laughter.

"Yes. He was trying to be incognito," she explained without explaining that he was a vampire himself.

"Or not! Anyway, this is so strange? The woman claims she was given a shot of something when she entered the country. Her and a bunch of other immigrants upon arrival?" Kim translated.

"Someone is running human trials!" Kristine suggested. It all started to make sense when she put it together. "We've been running into all kinds of strange mutations lately."

"And the American government is the common denominator!" the Korean offered. The line went silent for several moments while each pondered the ramifications of this development. If this was true then the same government paying them to eliminate vampires were also creating them.

CHAPTER 28

"Can you bring me some? Please!" Melcina pleaded when Prince and Kristine prepared to go feed. She had the taste of fresh blood once herself and longed for some more. The synthetic products and plasma were a cheap substitute.

"Um?" Prince paused to see how he could accommodate her request. Their child was in the next room sleeping or pretending to be sleep so they couldn't have a feeding frenzy in the living room.

"Sure. We'll bring you some take out," Kristine replied when a bright idea popped in her head. Prince shrugged and nodded since she obviously figured it out. They exited the apartment and headed down the hall.

"Up or down?" Prince asked when they reached the elevator bank.

"Up please," she answered with a wicked grin. He pressed the up call button to summon a car.

A few minutes later, the couple walked out on the roof and overlooked the magnificent city of New York. They both scanned the boroughs trying to decide which way to go. The sound of gunfire could be heard in all directions, so they settled on north.

Prince walked to the edge of the building and turned around. He cracked a fanged smile at his wife and let himself fall backwards. Kristine leaned over and watched as he plummeted down towards the concrete below. His wings sprang at the last second and he swooped high into the night air.

"Show off!" she called out and took flight after him. The couple swooped through Central Park and mingled with a flock of real bats. They dipped and dodged with the flying rodents for a few minutes then headed uptown.

Prince lagged back slightly so he could look at his wife's ass as they flew. She had a mean walk on her but seeing her butt in flight was downright spectacular.

"There!" she said and pointed below at a group of boys. The Bronx teens were roaming around with their dirty gun robbing and assaulting people.

"Dinner is served!" he said and followed her down. They landed a block ahead of the boys so they could stumble upon them.

"Man, that lady only had eight bucks!" the chubby leader named Chubs moaned in disgust. He was mad that the old woman they robbed only had a few bucks. It all went in his pocket since he was the leader. Only because he had the only gun and didn't mind shooting.

"I can't believe you shot her old ass!" another laughed hysterically. The other two joined in since their leader laughed. The hysteria came to a sudden stop when they turned the corner and saw the man and woman walking towards them

"Look y'all!" Chub said and looked both ways before pulling the rusty revolver.

"They look like they got money!" one of the sidekicks kicked. They certainly looked more well off than the old lady they just stuck up. They waited until they were right upon the couple before springing into action.

"Y'all know what it is!" Chub demanded and shoved the gun into Kristine's face.

"Can I have the fat one?" Kristine asked her husband as if he were a puppy in a window.

"Fat ones taste like cake with white icing," Prince advised. "With colorful sprinkles."

"Oh, I love sprinkles!" she cheered, clapped and bounced up and down. Her excitement quickly waned when she thought about the babysitter. "We'll save him for Melcina."

"Good idea," Prince said, totally ignoring the attempted robbery in progress.

"Um, excuse me, but we robbing y'all?" the sidekick said and waved his hand for attention. He would have been better off running for his life but it was too late.

"Excuse me, but we robbing y'all!" Kristine mocked and cracked her and her husband up.

"You think it's a game?" Chub snarled and fired at her. Kristine snatched the speeding bullet out of the air and looked at him.

"You have mommy issues. Did your mom not give you enough attention?" she asked sincerely.

"She probably propped his bottle on a pillow and went to play cards," Prince added. Chub wanted no parts of what was to come and took off. Kristine and Prince got a good laugh at the fat kid running for his but going nowhere fast.

They turned to his stunned friends and attacked. Screams filled the still night air as the two vampires fed on the three teens on the street. Prince watched on proudly as his ravenous wife fed from two while he devoured the third. She was becoming quite the animal and he was okay with that.

"Mmmm! Delish!" Kristine sang with a milk mustache made of blood.

"Don't forget, Melcina," Prince reminded and nodded ahead at the fat kid who had just made it to the corner.

"Help! Help me!" the boy pleaded and banged on the door of the corner store. He had been stealing out of this bodega since he was four years old and had no help coming from there.

"Adios!" the Puerto Rican papi laughed as the vampires descended on him.

Kristine snatched the chubby youth off of his feet and bolted upward into the sky. Chub fired his gun into her midsection as they ascended.

"You're tickling me!" she giggled at the bullets hitting her torso and flew away with him

"Well damn!" Prince exclaimed and took off after her. He caught up as they crossed the river back over Manhattan. Chub got a spectacular tour of the city one last time.

"I'll go get her," Prince said when they landed back on their own roof and went over the ledge.

"Show off," she fussed once more as he crawled down the side of the building like a gecko.

"Is he Spiderman?" the teen asked enthusiastically. The feat wasn't anymore bizarre than flying from the Bronx, but Spiderman excited him.

"No, he's not Spiderman!" she said and gave him a pop on the back of his head for asking the silly question. It was feeding time once again when Prince returned with Melcina a moment later.

"Uh oh!" Chub said when he saw the way the babysitter looked at him. Her fangs began to extend as she came near. He took off again but there was nowhere to run.

Prince and Kristine watched like proud lion parents as their cub made a kill. Melcina had only had human blood when A.J let her feed with him. This was her first kill and she was a natural.

"Nice," Prince nodded when she jumped on his back and bit his spine to end the pursuit. Chub fell and she landed on top of him.

Melcina turned Chub's head all the way around so his throat was facing her. She leaned in and took a huge bite of crime. Chub couldn't even struggle as she drained him dry.

"Taste like birthday cake!" she cheered, with blood dripping from her chin.

"With icing?" Kristine asked. She wanted a taste of her own now.

"And sprinkles!" Melcina nodded. Prince nodded too at the two of them. They were violent and thirsty just how he needed them.

*****

"This makes no sense!" Kristine said as she tried to make sense of what was going on.

"It makes perfect sense. You won't share the cure with them, so they are trying to make one of their own," Prince concluded. The cure was worth billions and governments would rather make the money than spend it.

"Immigration?" she asked and shook her head. "No, they're using the immigrants as guinea pigs."

"And causing all sorts of mutations as a result!" Prince growled. That made for unstable creatures who were getting harder to kill. Others like the hotdog lady had traces of vampire that could be detected even if they weren't actually vampires. The lines were deliberately being blurred. Now they needed to find out who.

"This has to end!" Kristine declared as she thought about the ramifications.

"This will end!" he assured her since he intended to end it. "Meanwhile..."

"Yeah, I know," she pouted and twisted her lips. She had stalled and procrastinated long enough. It was time to draw their son's blood so it could be analyzed.

"I know what that means," Prince said with a pout and a sigh.

"That makes no sense whatsoever! You're the only vampire on the planet who doesn't like needles!"

It was true but Prince knew what he had to do. He rolled up his sleeve so he could lead by example. He joined his son playing video games and sat down beside him.

"Sup, pops," the little New Yorker greeted with a head nod, but without taking his eyes off the screen.

"Just chilling, homie," he said and grabbed a controller to join him. As planned, Kristine came out a few minutes later in her lab coat.

"Hey, guys. I need to get blood samples from you both," she said clinically so she wouldn't get any lip.

"I better go first. Dad is scared of needles," Martin offered and stuck out his arm. " See, it don't hurt."

"I see," Prince said as Kristine extracted one vial then another. She removed the needle and watched the needle hole close instantly. She still placed a Band-Aid on it and sealed it with a kiss.

"Next," she said and turned to her husband.

"Next what? You don't even need mine now!" he protested, but she wasn't trying to hear it.

"Come on, mister man!" she insisted and pulled his arm. Prince winced when she stuck the needle in and she twisted her lips. "Can you even feel this?"

"No. It's just a flash back from when I was a kid," he explained.

"That was seventy years ago!" she fussed as she filled the vials. His pinhole closed the second she pulled the needle out as well. She had what she needed and rushed into her lab to get back to work.

*****

"Okay. Let's see what we have here!" Kristine mumbled to herself as she looked at her son's blood under the microscope. She couldn't believe what she was seeing, so she moved over to the electro-microscope for a closer look.

"This is amazing!" she marveled at her findings. The boy's blood was all vampire and totally indestructible. She put a tiny amount in with a sample of vampire blood and it began to spark and killed it instantly. Even the smallest drop was deadly to the vampire virus. The boy was the kill.

"Let's try this," Kristine wondered aloud and put her husband's blood in a test tube, followed by a drop of her son's. The results were astonishing. The mix of father and son's blood turned into a super-charged mixture.

Young Martin was the most dangerous person on the planet. She added it to human blood and it turned into vampire blood instantly. The reality scared her to the core.

"Prince!" she shouted urgently out the door.

"Uh oh. You're in trouble! What you do?" little Marin said when he heard her tone.

"I 'on know. Come with me," Prince asked as he stood.

"You're on your own buddy," the child said and retreated to his own room.

"I don't know what you think I did or broke, but Martin did it," he said as he entered the room. The joke was abandoned when he saw the look of sheer horror on her face. "What?"

"Watch this," she said and showed him what she discovered. She repeated all the tests, so he could see the results for himself.

"No wonder she's after him!" Prince said when he took it all in. This made things even more urgent than ever. If whoever was behind the experiments got wind of this they would come after their son, as well. "You know what this means?"

No sooner did they leave the mixture of father and son's blood, it began to bubble, spark and then died. He was the cure and the kill.

CHAPTER 29

"We have to get stronger. We must get stronger!" Prince announced urgently.

"You seem pretty strong to me!" his wife said breathlessly since he just knocked her boots to the moon and back.

"Yeah, well," he blushed at the compliment. He shook the flattery away and got back to the subject at hand. The new revelations had him worried and he had to protect his family. That meant they both had to get stronger.

"Family trip," Kristine said and reminded him of the upcoming vampire retreat in Detroit. It would host hundreds of vampires and wannabe vampires in one place.

"Let's bring Melcina along," he suggested. She was part of the family now since she and Martin had bonded like siblings.

"Yes. She needs to be stronger, too!" Kristine agreed since the babysitter was with their child in their frequent absences.

With that set, the family traveled by night to the iconic city of Detroit. Vampires were on the rise there as well and were causing problems. Each of the burned out shells of homes were littered with empty corpses of humans caught after sundown. With winter approaching, that meant the streets were deserted before five PM.

"At least there are no more crack heads roaming around," Kristine mused as Prince drove through the city. Their presence turned heads when vampires felt their presence.

"Good. I don't care for the taste anyway," he said and scrunched his face. He may have been impervious to the diseases and drugs in their system, but it gave their blood a foul taste. Similar to spoiled milk. They cruised the city in search of bad people to make a good meal of. Meanwhile, back at the hotel, dinner came to Melcina.

*****

188

"Go to the room," Melcina directed in response to a soft knock on the door of their suite.

"Okay," the obedient child said and complied. She waited until the door closed behind him before popping her fangs and claws out.

"Who!" she growled as she unlocked the door and took a step back.

"Um, Dennis. I'm the bellhop. I brought your bags up earlier," the creepy man called through the door. Melcina frowned even deeper as she recalled his eyes roaming all over her and Kristine as he delivered their bags to the room. Prince saw it too and planned to deal with him before they left, but he wasn't going to make it that long. It didn't look like he was going to make it through the night.

"How can I help you, Dennis?" Melcina asked as she opened the door minus the fangs and claws so she wouldn't scare him off.

"I saw your parents leave. Thought you might wanna hang out? Get a bite to eat?" he asked as his eyes ran up and down.

"I would love a bite to eat!" she admitted. She could feel and hear the pulse of his heart beating through his chest. Martin let out a shout at losing a life on his video game, which meant he was good and occupied. Melcina looked back at the bedroom door before stepping out into the hallway.

"I wanna eat, too," Dennis suggested with a suggestive nod below her waist.

"You won't after I get through with you!" she promised and let him lead her away. The employees had a spare room they used to do dirt, so that's where he escorted her.

"In here," he said as he opened the door and stepped aside. He grabbed a handful of booty as she passed by. It would be a going away present since she attacked as soon as the door closed behind them.

Melcina let out a loud hiss as her fangs and claws came back out. His eyes went wide when he realized that he had invited death into his life. He made a move for the door, but it was too little too late.

Once again, she went for his spine and disabled her prey. There was nothing he could do as she drained him completely dry.

*****

"Remember to bring some take out back for Melcina," Kristine reminded as she watched a Chinese man stepped out the back of a Chinese restaurant.

"Mmhm," Prince said and kept an eye out for their dinner. He parked in the hood in hopes someone would come along doing something they shouldn't so he could eat them. Meanwhile, she kept a curious eye of the cook.

"What the—" she frowned when he retrieved two cats from pens kept in the alley. He snapped their necks and took them back inside. "I just found dinner!"

"I'm not eating no cat!" Prince protested.

"Sure you are. As soon as we get home. Now come with me," she directed and hopped out. He knew she was right about him eating some cat when they got back, so he shut up and followed her inside.

"Chicken fry rice? Fresh!" the woman at the counter sang along with the bell over the door. Meanwhile, the man in back was using one of the many, many ways to skin the cats he just killed.

"Chicken or cat?" Kristine dared. The slant eyed lady squinted and checked for health department badges.

"You like cat I make for you," she said as if it were a secret.

"See, that's why I always ordered wings. Cats don't have wings," Prince said just before he turned.

"Word," his wife said and turned, too. Screams filled the night air as the vampire couple leapt the counter and fed.

Prince thought it ironic to skin the cook first and hang him upside down along with the cats. He slit his throat with his fangs and feasted until the man went dry.

Kristine took the traditional route and bit deeply into the woman's neck. She struggled and flailed which only made her heart beat that much faster. Her blood flowed that much quicker and she was drained dry that much sooner.

"We forgot Melcina!" Kristine said and snapped her fingers when they got back to the car.

"I'm sure we can find—" Prince began but was interrupted by the unmistakable sound of a backhanded pimpslap echoing through the night air.

"What the fuck is this!" the pimp demanded and threw the few dollars back in the girl's face.

"May, I?" Kristine asked. Her husband gave a nod and she pulled the door handle.

"I'll see you back at the hotel," Prince said and pulled away. Kristine turned into a black blur and sped towards the man.

"Bi—" the pimp was saying before being scooped into the air and swooped away.

"I can't hear you?" the girl laughed but didn't laugh long. A pack of young vampires came out of an alley and spotted her. She spotted them too and made a run for it. They quickly tracked her down and fed on her.

"Wait here," Kristine told the man when she landed on the roof. It wasn't much of a request since she snapped his legs like twigs so he couldn't escape.

Melcina had sensed her presence when she neared the door. "I brought you some... what did you do?"

"Well, I got hungry and he came knocking and..." Melcina lowered her head and admitted. Kristine got the rest of the story from the girl's head and shook her own.

"Well, we may as well have seconds," she said. She poked her head in to peek at her sleeping child before leading her up to the roof.

"What have we here?" Melcina asked when she saw the flamboyantly dressed man. He was crawling to the stairs, trying to get away before the vampire came back. To make matters worse, two vampires came back.

"Pimpjuice!" Kristine laughed. Melcina did too and both bared their fangs.

"Guess it's dinner time," Prince laughed when he heard the shrill scream as he approached the hotel. It died in the man's throat when a vampire latched on to each side of his neck. There was nothing left to do except shut up and die, so that's what he did.

Of course he was tasked with disposing of the empties when they were done feeding. After all, taking out the trash is men's work.

*****

"I wish I could go!" Melcina pouted as the night began to overtake the day.

"You are going," Kristine said to her surprise. "I arranged for a sitter. This won't take long,"

"Not long at all," Prince seconded when he came out dressed to impress. He wanted to make a grand impression even though no one would live to remember it.

"I'll go get dressed!" she cheered and rushed into the room.

"I better get dressed, too," little Martin said, not wanting to be left out.

"Not this time, little man. Miss Andrews is coming to hang out with you," his mother said soothingly. She had found her in the network of vampire sympathizers. The sweet lady campaigned for vampire rights. Little did she know, there could be only one and Prince and Kristine planned to kill all the rest.

"That must be her," Prince said of the knock on the door. Answering it was men's work too in the Jones home, so he went to pull it open.

"Well, hello! Aren't you guys handsome!" the woman gushed and hugged Prince tightly. He gave her mind a scan and found no malice. Just butterflies and lillies.

"Hello, Mrs. Andrews," Kristine greeted and ran a background check through her mind as well.

Once the niceties were out the way, the trio of vampires set off for the vampire jamboree. The party was held in one of the city's new casinos. Fitting since being a vampire was a real gamble.

"We're set?" Prince asked after going over the plans once more on the drive over. Kristine wanted to fly, but Melcina didn't have the ability just yet. They would all have new powers after dispatching the thousand vampires expected.

"Set!" both women said and bared their fangs. Prince pulled up to the valet and got out.

"Mortal," he surmised of the attendant who took the car away. They would try to separate vampires from mortals but couldn't make any guarantees. This would be a slaughter. There would be collateral damage amongst would be vampires.

"If you wanna scramble eggs, you have to break a few shells," Kristine said with a shrug. She didn't read his mind they were just on the same page.

"Legs and heads, too," he agreed.

"This is crazy!" Melcina marveled as they walked inside. She had stars in her eyes when she looked around the festivities.

There were turning booths instead of tanning booths so people could make the leap from mortal to immortal. They had to sign a waiver of course ,plus no one mentioned that there could be only one. Vampires could only socialize but for so long before turning on each other. The savvy vampires amongst them were making list of victims to kill so they could add to their powers.

Vampires are licentious creators and several copulated with each other or mortals. Kristine wondered at the results of any babies conceived. None would be like her own since none of these vampires had Prince's powers. Still she couldn't take any chances and let them be born.

Both human and vampire blood was being served at the bar. Kristine scrunched her face at the dangerous display. Humans couldn't be turned from the vampire blood unless they were first bitten. It did create a euphoria better than any drug on the market. She had no way of knowing which ones were bitten and which ones were not. She just shrugged and lumped them all in together.

"Well take your positions. Let's get the party started," Prince ordered. Melcina merged into the gyrating sea of bodies on the dance floor. Kristine mingled over to the blood bar to wait on the signal. Prince never said what the signal would be. Only that they would know it when they saw it.

A mash up rock/hip hop band was on the stage pumping out rage music. The partygoers bounced around the dance floor like human pinballs. Some humans were left lumped and bloody from the violence on the dance floor.

"You can't come on stage," a vampire bouncer advised as Prince climbed the back stairs to go back stage.

Prince was polite enough to let him get it out before politely biting his throat away. He held the struggling man as his life's blood gushed from the open wound into his open mouth.

"Refreshing!" Prince declared as he felt the surge of power enter his body. The bouncer had obviously been feeding on other vampires because he could feel the rush of the dead souls.

Playtime came to a sudden end when he suddenly morphed into his wolf-like creature. The crowd roared with applause when he bounded out and bit the lead guitarist, guitar and all, completely in half. They "oohed" and "aahed" at what they thought were some really special, special effects.

The crowd went curiously quiet when Prince turned to the front man and bit his head off. The bass player knew this wasn't part of the act and tried to make a run for it. He didn't get far before the wolf pounced on his back and began to eat him.

"Showoff!" Kristine said and shook her head.

The stunned audience finally caught on and caught out. Tried to anyway because both women pulled their weapons. Melcina lacked the training, so she wielded a cross bow. The poisoned tipped stakes made quick work of vampires and humans.

Kristine took a deep breath and transformed into a blur. She drew her claws and sped around the venue slashing, biting, and stabbing. The wolf ran around the perimeter making sure no one escaped. The mist of blood hung in the air like London fog and the death toll increased.

Kristine felt the surge of power with each vampire life she took. She knew they were mortal if she felt nothing. Still she felt nothing as she killed mortal and immortal alike.

"Showoff," Prince said to himself when he transformed back to himself. He watched proudly like a lion king watching his lionesses making a kill. The chaos slowly came to and end when the women ran out of victims. They roamed around looking for any signs of life and snuffed them out.

This was a turning point for Prince and Kristine. Both felt the effects of absorbing so many lives. Tonight would put the vampire world on notice. So much so, even Katrina noticed.

"Let's get out of here," Prince said once their work was done.

"Let's!" Kristine agreed out loud, while Melcina nodded. Melcina drove while the couple took to the air. The large bats fluttered back to the hotel and landed on the roof. They walked down to their floor and entered the room.

"We're back!" Kristine sang as Prince opened the door and stepped aside for his queen to enter. The smile disappeared when she saw her child alone on the sofa playing his game.

"Where's Mrs. Andrews?" Prince asked as he rushed inside and looked around.

"Gone," the little boy said and kept on playing.

"Gone where?" his mother demanded and stepped in front of him. Martin quickly paused the game instead of asking her to move. He didn't get many spankings but that was the quickest way to get one.

"I'on know, ma. She took my blood then left," he shrugged.

CHAPTER 30

Martin looked down at the hands holding his hands, then smiled up at the owners of those hands. It had been months since both parents had taken him to the park in the middle of the day. It was the dead of winter but no one seemed to mind in the least.

"Beautiful day for a stroll, Mr. Jones," Kristine sang and looked directly at the once deadly sun.

"It is, Mrs. Jones," Prince agreed. The massacre in Detroit had turned them both into daywalkers and more. Melcina still had a ways to go but was still more powerful than most vampires. She was adequate protection for their son while they made their rounds around the country killing strays.

The massacre served to drive the vampires back into the shadows. It was no longer safe to flaunt being undead since Mr. and Mrs. Jones would come make you dead-dead.

Prince wore an "I wish she would" smirk on his face in hopes Katrina would pop up like she did in England. Kristine was ready, just not as eager. The fact that someone had her son's blood unnerved her. It was the most dangerous substance she'd ever come across. Now only God knows who had it and only God knows for what. That's why she prayed since only God could guide her.

The family enjoyed a frigid family outing before Prince went on a mission the next day. He had a slew of new tricks up his sleeves and couldn't wait to try them out.

Likewise, Kristine had some new powers of her own. She had a mission of her own locally. They spent the night pleasing each other before Prince set off for Ohio. Each had a promising lead to follow up on.

*****

"Welcome to America!" a happy emigrant sang as the plane landed. He said it again as they lined up for customs check. The man was pretty well off in his native Guyana but sold it all for passage to America.

"Excuse me, you. Yes, you. Step out of line for additional screening," a customs agent directed and directed him into a room. He joined the other curious passengers waiting for screening. Most prayed to whoever they prayed to not to get sent back. To their relief, they only received a quick medical exam and vaccination.

"What exactly is this?" an elderly lady asked when the nurse approached her with a syringe filled with a murky liquid.

"Passage into America. Unless you wanna go back to your rice paddy!" the woman barked. She was all bark but no bite when the elderly lady began to get younger right before her eyes. She went from Asian to a mixed Egyptian black in a few seconds.

"I'll ask you again," Kristine asked politely. She could afford to be sweet since her long fangs were anything but.

"I don't know what's in it! I get paid a hundred bucks for every positive reaction!" she blurted and gave Kristine the whole story. And what a story it was.

"What government? This government?" she asked incredulously.

"America!" the nurse shot back like, "who else". She wasn't particularly patriotic, but America would be her last words.

Kristine struck with the speed of light and bit into her throat. She squirmed and struggled which only shortened her struggle. The vampire greedily slurped down the woman's blood.

"Give your bosses a message," she told the corpse as she left if behind. She and Prince usually disposed of their victims to stay under the radar. Now they left a trail of corpses as a calling card. They were the hunters and the hunted.

*****

Mrs. Andrews awoke and took a hearty old lady pee to start her day. She popped her smile in her mouth and stepped out of the bathroom to fix her morning cup of coffee. She only made it two steps before stopping dead in her tracks when she came face to face with herself.

"Huh?" she asked and squinted at the mirror image of her own image.

"Huh?" her other self asked and mocked her movements. Her reflection raised its hand when she did. They both waved right then left. The reflection broke ranks and delivered a mighty slap that knocked her smile back into the bathroom and her into her wide ass.

"You!" Mrs. Andrews said to her other self when she turned into the Dark Prince. Both he and Kristine could now shift into almost any shape they wanted.

"Me," he growled and transformed halfway into the wolf. "Where is my son's blood? Who sent you?"

Mrs. Andrews wanted to lie but the large animal above with drool dripping from it's foot long fangs were better than the best truth serum. She would rather tell the truth than be eaten.

"A company in Washington! You won't give them the cure, so they decided to take it. They think your child is the link between humans and vampires!" she rattled on until she ended at the Washington DC lab being where she delivered the vial of blood to.

Prince slowly transformed back into his whole self but was no less scary. The woman watched hopefully from below as he pondered their situation. His next stop was Washington DC but who was next? When would it end? Would his child be safe? What he did know was she had to die. The claws on one hand popped out and took her head off with one quick swipe. He watched it roll away and plotted his next move.

*****

"Humph," Kristine huffed when Prince shared his finding. She shared what she found out and pondered their situation. DC was first but what was next?

"We have to keep him close. They will come for him!" Prince threw into the equation. If it wasn't bad enough to have Katrina on their heels, they now had to worry about the government.

"DC is just a lab. Homeland Security has to be behind this," she surmised since that was who they dealt with to cure or kill the country's vampire population.

"They haven't asked for the formula in weeks!" Prince added. That was rare since they had been asking daily. "That's how they knew we would be in Detroit!"

"Well, they don't know we'll be in Washington. It's time to pay them a visit!" she said and let her fangs hang.

"Put those up before you scare the children," he reminded as their child ran and played with other children. Young Martin still showed no outward signs of being a vampire except for reading minds. Even that was dangerous in the wrong hands.

"Come on, baby! Time to go home," she called and collected her child. They called Melcina on the way home so they could all make the trip to DC.

Kristine went straight to her lab to work on her latest weapon. They wanted her son's blood son bad she was going to give it to them. She came with the idea of delivering it as they set off on I-95 south.

"I can't wait until I can walk around in the sun!" Melcina pouted once the vibration of the vehicle rocked the kid to sleep. The heavy tint on the car allowed her to remove the layers of clothing she wore to ward off the sun rays.

"Be patient. You will. There are plenty vampires left to kill. Then, there will be only three, not one!" Kristine replied. She knew they could all live in peace once all the rest were dead. "We just have to stay under the radar until this is done."

"Not sure how long that's going to last," Prince sighed as he made an abrupt lane changed while watching the rearview. His head shook when the three matching SUVs changed with him.

"Who is that?" Kristine asked. She got the answer to her question when she saw the identical tinted out vehicles behind them. "So much for low key!"

"You drive while I—" Prince was saying until Kristine opened the passenger door and jumped out. The vehicle was doing almost a hundred miles an hour, but she didn't stumble or fall. Instead, she took off running full speed at the first vehicle.

"I got it!" Melcina offered as she climbed from the backseat to take the wheel.

Prince watched in amazement when his wife jumped and dove head first into their first vehicle. Her claws and fangs spread as she penetrated the windshield. She flew through the truck and out the back window along with the heads of the four occupants.

"Show off!" Prince said below as he flew over her. He landed in front of the next vehicle and lowered his shoulder. The truck crumbled against his body like it hit a concrete barrier. It somersaulted overhead and landed on it top. Kristine landed on it's underside and punched through the gas tank.

The last truck came to a screeching halt when the second truck exploded. The driver slammed the SUV in reverse and floored it. The vampire hunting couple of vampires looked at each other, then took off after it.

"What the fuck!" the driver screamed when they caught up and ran along side the vehicle travelling sixty miles an hour in reverse.

"They said we just had to follow them!" one of the men in the back moaned. That is despite the HK-MP5 on his lap.

"Roll it down," Prince said through the glass, while making the motion with his hand.

"Un uh! Don't roll it down!" the passenger screamed. He had a machine gun as well but knew it was useless after Prince just flipped a whole truck over with his shoulder. He turned his head and saw Kristine running along the other side of the truck.

"Let's see what he wants," the driver said since he couldn't outrun them. He rolled it down and cracked a friendly smile even though he was weaving through traffic backwards. "Um, hey?"

"Who do you work for?" Prince asked.

"Not allowed to say," the driver said since they weren't allowed to say. Prince just peered into his brain and got the answer from his mind, then attacked.

Prince snatched the driver out of the open window and tossed him into oncoming traffic on the other side of the highway. A big rig quickly put him out of his misery as it rolled over him with eight of its eighteen wheels.

Kristine refused to be outdone and snatched the passenger door off. The passenger turned his gun on her and opened fire. She opened her mouth and swallowed like she did with her husband.

"My turn!" she said like she did when she was at home with her husband. Except this time she spit those same nine millimeter rounds back with just as much velocity. Prince put his shoulder down once again and nudged the truck off the highway. It rolled down the embankment and burst into flames.

Prince and Kristine let their wings out and took off into the air. They scanned both sides of the highway for potential threats, but found none. They spotted their own vehicle still moving and quickly caught up with it.

They climbed back into the open window and came face to face with their child. Young Martin blinked in disbelief and his parents had some 'splaining to do.

CHAPTER 31

"You see, son..." Prince began. It was time to say something to the shocked boy when they finally made it to DC. What to say was the question.

"Mommy and daddy are different," Kristine added and nodded as if she just solved it. Her son squinted at her then turned back to his father.

"Different," he cosigned and looked towards his wife.

"I think I understand," Martin said. The boy's IQ was through the roof, so he picked up things rather quickly. He had yet to start kindergarten but was already reading at a college level.

"You do?" his mother asked eagerly. She was ready to put it to bed so they could handle the business they came for.

"Yes. Daddy is Batman! And you're Bat Girl!" the child cheered with the enthusiasm of childhood.

"Yes!" both parents shouted together. It was no worse than Santa and the Easter bunny lies they told already. One day they would just explain everything at once.

"Okay, that's cool. I'm not judging," the kid said and went to hook up his game systems. Who was he to judge anyway when he had secrets of his own?

"That went well!" Prince said, declaring victory.

"No. No, it did not," Kristine laughed and shook her head. They both stood as well and got ready for their mission.

Being shape shifters saved time on disguises since they could change appearance in an instant. It backfired at times when Kristine would morph into an old Jewish lady while they made love. Prince got her back by turning into the 45th president. Not even Mrs. Trump wants to sleep with Mr. Trump.

They followed the directions they gleamed from the minds of the driver of the truck and found themselves in front on a nondescript building. Kristine could tell by discrete sounds and smells that a lab was located inside.

"Tight security. I don't want to cause a scene until we find the lab," Prince said as they watched from across the street.

"And once we do, I'm going to make a scene alright a crime scene!" Kristine growled and bared her fangs.

"Easy. You know you turn me on when you growl like that!" he growled back. They shared a kiss that could have led to more if two guards hadn't come out of the building on their way to lunch.

"Rain check!" she offered and hopped out. He got out and followed her across the street. They transformed into the same guards who just pulled away.

"You guys back already?" another guard asked as he buzzed them inside.

"Yeah. I forgot my umm, and the..." Prince said over his shoulder as he led the way inside.

"Up," Kristine said as she read the signs. They entered the elevator and rode up to the top floor.

"Vampires!" Prince said as the doors opened. He felt the presence before the doors opened. Both of their eyes went wide when they saw at least fifty newly made vampires.

"What the—" Kristine said when she saw rows of vampires strapped to gurneys in a separate room. The domes over the beds were like incubators. They were breeding vampires.

"You handle that. I'll get them," Prince said and nodded towards a bunch of scientist in another lab. They nodded and went their separate ways.

Kristine went into her bag of tricks and came out with what looked like a smoke bomb. She opened the door, ignited it, and tossed it inside. She quickly shut it before the deadly fumes could reach her. While their son's blood could supercharge her and Prince, it was instant death for normal vampires. It would kill them too once the effects wore off. A fact she kept from her husband until she could figure out a way to fix it.

Kristine braced herself for the rush that came with each vampire kill. This many at once might knock her off her feet. Yet nothing came. The synthetic vampires were too new and too weak to transfer any powers.

"Excuse me?" Prince called out as he stepped into the secure lab. The lab rats inside looked more perturbed by the interruption than his presence.

"Another one got out," one of the scientist sighed. Their unwilling participants tried to escape every chance they got.

"I got it," one said with a sigh and grabbed a syringe. He took one step towards Prince but Prince tapped him on his shoulder from behind.

"Psst," Prince whispered and turned the man's head completely around to face him. The crunch of bones and cartilage turned all heads. The gory sight set off a panic as they rushed for the door.

Kristine watched proudly as the black blur sped around the room, turning the windows and walls red with blood. Prince felt no thirst but still sampled some of the blood he shed. He was a vampire after all and it was blood. She took the opportunity to overload all systems. Then unhooked the gas lines and removed the hard drives from computers.

"Let's go!" she shouted once she had what she needed. There were a couple of scientists left alive but no more time. They both ran for the windows and leapt through just as the building exploded. The force of the blast behind them hurled them high into the air. They spread their wings and flew back towards their hotel.

"Someone's gonna be big mad!" she said of the inferno behind them.

"Yup. At least we won't have to go looking for them anymore," Prince said, then added the ominous reason. "They're gonna come looking for us!"

*****

"Have fun and be safe," Kristine advised as Melcina prepared to go out for the night. A group of wannabe vampires came across her social media feed, so she made a date to go be social and feed.

"Come with!" she asked excitedly. "Martin is with his dad. They won't even miss you!"

"You think?" Kristine asked in hopes of being talked into it. Besides, she could eat.

"I'm sure! Plus, it'll be fun. Girls night out!" she said and sealed the deal. Prince nodded and grunted when she filled him in on their plans for the evening. He and his son were engaged in a heated game of Madden and didn't need the interruption.

"He'll swear I didn't say anything to him," Kristine said as they set out of the hotel and into the night.

"Race you," Melcina dared and took off. She couldn't fly but could run with the wind. Kristine laughed and let her get a few blocks lead. One mighty leap and she landed in front of her when she reached the storefront church the wannabes used as a meeting place.

"Almost!" Kristine laughed at the look of frustration on her face. "Don't worry, chica. You'll get stronger."

"Maybe tonight," she said as the presence of a vampire inside reached them.

"Maybe," Kristine replied and led the way inside. They both stifled a laugh at the fuckery inside.

"Blood of Jesus," the vampire/preacher said and passed a chalice around.

"Did he say, Heysues?" Melcina asked of the Latino pronunciation of Jesus.

"He did," kristine laughed. The presence of two real vampires lifted Jesus's head.

"We have guest! Greetings!" he greeted. "Welcome to the church of Heysues!"

"Mmhm. Just what lies are you telling these people?" Kristine asked since she could see they were all still mortal. All nefarious types in search of powers to advance their debauchery. They were night people who did dirt under the cover of darkness.

"Lies? Lies!" Heysues boomed and laughed. He had a charisma that attracted the hundred people sitting in his pews. "I'm offering eternal life! Who wants to live forever?"

"Meee!" a hundred voices called and two hundred hands raised.

"Live forever, huh?" Melcina laughed. "Drink that blood and you're dying tonight!"

"Yup!" Kristine cosigned when she saw the bite marks on their necks. The slick vampire fed off his congregation for free. Now he would turn them so he could kill them and absorb their powers.

"Lies!" Heysues challenged. He lifted his challis and his flocked lifted theirs. He turned his up and they did the same.

"Can't say we ain't warn 'em," Melcina shrugged. Kristine opened her mouth to agree but got stuck when the mortals turned to immortals instantly.

"Martin's blood!" she surmised when the humans instantly turned into vampires. Both women pulled their silver swords and attacked.

Arms, legs and heads tumbled in the air as they slashed their way through the church. Heysues wasn't the sharpest tool in the shed but knew enough to make a run for it.

"I got him! You finish them!" Kristine said and took off after him. He went out the back door and she went after him. She took a leap and landed in front of him in the alley.

"Hey! Hey! Be easy! I'm just tryna eat!" Heysues pleaded with his hands out.

"I get it. We cool. No problem," she said understandingly. "I just need to know where you got that blood from?"

"I'm not saying!" he said defiantly. Pretty much like Kristine figured. That's why she asked the question so he would think of the answer. He didn't need to say it outloud since she could go inside his mind and get it.

"Thanks!" she nodded and bit a chunk out of his chest. She reached in and snatched out his beating heart. There was an awkward silence as they both looked at the organ in her hand. "Have some?"

Heysues blinked twice and died once. Kristine shrugged and took a bite like it was a crisp apple. She turned and walked back into the church. It looked nothing like it did when she left. Body parts littered the floor, walls, and even the ceiling. Melcina sat back rubbing her bloated belly and picking meat from her fangs.

"Done?" Kristine asked as she looked around.

"Done!" she said and followed her out. It was time to go home.

CHAPTER 32

"Here?" Prince asked and squinted at the building in front of them. The family health clinic treated the city's poor and needy. A perfect pool of people to experiment on.

"This is what he said. Well thought out," Kristine said. This was the place Heysues said he acquired Martin's blood. She confirmed it was the real deal when she found traces of it left in the challis. It was diluted but the real deal.

"Well let's go inside," he said and led the way. They couple transformed into a disheveled elderly couple and limped inside.

"Can we get some help? My husband feeling sick!" Kristine wailed when they walked through the door. She saw the nurse's eyes light up when she spotted them. They were the perfect patients for their new client.

A large pharmaceutical company kicked them a nice kick back for every person they hooked on their products. It was the opioid epidemic all over again except they were making synthetic vampires to sell their synthetic cures to.

The nurses looked at the elderly couple then at each other. Their eyes lit up with dollar signs at the two new patients to pawn the drugs on. They had no idea what the end results were and didn't care. The company paid per head and two more heads just walked in.

"Right back here," one said with glee and escorted them to the rear.

"Feel that?" The elderly Prince asked when they reached the hall-way.

"My baby," Kristine snared. She almost blew her cover when her fangs slid past the old lady lips. Luckily, the greedy nurse was too eager to inject her with the new drug and didn't see.

"Looks like the flu. I better treat you both," she suggested and retrieved a vial made from the blood stolen from their son. They could

209

both feel the essence of the boy in the vial. Proof of just how power-ful and potent their child was.

"We have a treat for you!" Kristine cheered as her and Prince turned into her and Prince. The woman's eyes went wide with ques-tions that she would never get the answer to. Instead, the vampires shared her blood like young lovers sipping one drink from two straws. Except in this case each took a jugular vein and sucked her dry.

The second nurse entered and became desert. Both separated and searched the clinic. Workers became snacks while they spared the patients. They were going to need a new clinic though because this one was closed.

"Find anything?" Prince asked when they met back up outside.

"The rest of this," Kristine replied and held up the vials of solu-tion made from Martin's blood. She looked at the company infor-mation on the box and found the source. "Looks like we're going to Denver."

*****

"Kill the head and the body will die," Prince said as the family trav-eled to Colorado. They tracked the owners down to California. They planned to pay them a visit soon but first stop was Denver.

"Yes," Kristine agreed and cast a glance at her child in the back seat. She would give her life to keep him safe. A soft smile spread on her face knowing that Melcina sleeping beside him would give hers, as well. So would her husband, but she would kill the rest of the world to keep it from coming to that.

"I'm hungry," Melcina pouted when she blinked awake in con-junction with the setting sun.

"We'll stop soon so we can grab a bite," Prince offered. The truck stops that littered the nations highways were always good for a quick meal. They were filled with rogue truck drivers and lounge lizards who no one would miss. They were the fast food for a family of vampires.

"There," Kristine said and pointed at the golden arches high above. On cue, their son popped his head up like he could sense the happy meals ahead. He could he could sense a lot of things.

"I'm on it," Prince said and switched lanes so he could exit. There was plenty of activity around the parked trucks and Melcina licked her lips in anticipation.

"I'll take him inside," Kristine offered when they pulled in front of the restaurant. She took Martin by the hand and led him inside while Prince and Melcina headed for the parked trucks.

"Mmm, I want him!" Melcina sang when an obese trucker waddled by. He was shoving donuts into his mouth from a box of a dozen as if they were potato chips.

"Too sweet for me," Prince said and scrunched his face. He spotted a lounge lizard slither by and licked his lips. They bumped fist and went in different directions.

"Looking for a good time?" the addict asked when Prince approached.

"I am!" he said and bared his fangs. The woman realized she was in trouble and took off running. Prince walked at a slow pace and followed her to the source. She ran directly to her pimps car and hopped in the passenger seat.

"What the hell wrong with you? And where is my money?" was all he wanted to know. She was too scared for words and could only point. "A vampire? You scared of a vampire!"

The man grabbed his trusty vampire repellant kit. He just paid $99.99 on Amazon and couldn't wait to give it a try.

"Uh oh!" Prince said and stopped in his tracks when the man appeared with his bag of tricks.

"Un uh! Too late now!" the pimp laughed and prepped his cross-bow. He paused to read the directions and Prince waited. "Okay, I got it now."

"Nooo," Prince wailed when he aimed and sent wooden stakes his way. They hit their target and down went Prince just like the directions said. All that was left was the final stake through the heart.

"See how I did that!" the pimp bragged to his hoe and stepped forward to deliver the coup de gras. He lifted the stake high and brought it down with all his might towards Prince's heart. Instead it broke against the asphalt below. "Huh?"

"That's not in the directions, huh?" Prince asked from behind him. The man's head shook before it tumbled into the air from a swipe of Prince's claws.

The woman's eyes went wide when Prince turned her headless pimp completely upside down and let his blood run into his mouth. She has seen enough and hopped back out to run for her life.

"Wait!" Prince demanded and stopped her dead in her tracks. Her mind was telling her limbs to keep moving but they had a new master. She was stuck in place even after he walked away.

Meanwhile, Melcina caught up with her dinner. She strolled past the man's rig and he popped his head out to catch her. The young, clean woman looked nothing like the stragglers and strays who roamed the truck stop.

"Hey there, little lady! Can I get a date?" he asked and popped another donut into his face.

"I would love a date!" Melcina sang and climbed into his cab. He led the way into the sleeper compartment and closed the partition.

The whole truck began to rock and shake when she attacked. The little man put up a big fight since his life was on the line. He lost that fight when she sank her fangs into the layers of fat protecting his jugular.

"Mmm!" she cheered when a rush of sweet, sugary blood flooded her mouth. Her feet did the happy food dance below as she literally sucked the life out of the man. She reached the bottom of his barrel at the same time Prince reached his family inside the restaurant.

"Did you save me some?" Kristine asked when Prince returned.

"On ice next to the black Lincoln," he said and switched places with her.

Martin switched his chatter from his mother to his father when he slid into the booth. Kristine skipped happily along towards her dinner until she saw the car in question.

The skinny addict was still stuck in place but Kristine overlooked her in hopes her husband picked a better meal than that. Addicts had an aftertaste she could do with out.

"Um, you can go," she said and sent the woman scurrying along her way. Her senses went on high alert when she sensed another vampire in the vicinity. It just so happened to select the truck stop for the same reasons they were here. A quick, disposable meal similar to what was being slung under those golden arches.

"What the—" the addict fussed when she got snatched up into a truck as she ran. Kristine's fangs extended their full length as she approached.

The feeding vampire felt her presence but it was too late.

"What the—" he said as Kristine came crashing through the windshield. The predator became prey when she clamped down on his neck. She bit his throat away down to the spine and began to drink. The woman was spared for a second time in one night.

"Fuck this shit!" she decided as she escaped. She was taking her ass back home where she belonged. The streets had sufficiently kicked her ass and she was done.

"Mmm," Kristine moaned as she reached the bottom of the vampire. She could feel his energy flowing into her. She could only hope it added a new trick to her bag of tricks. Prince had a big headstart on her, but she hoped to catch up one day.

CHAPTER 33

"Humph," Kristine huffed at the results of her latest experiment. The diluted blood solution turned people into vampires just as quickly. However, it supercharged her and Prince's blood without the lethal affects as the pure blood.

The results only lasted momentarily, reverting back to normal. It would be good for a quick boost, if needed. She fixed emergency syringes of both the diluted blood as well as the pure just in case. She and Prince had evolved and she was too smart to believe that Melcina hadn't, as well.

"Ready?" Prince asked as he stuck his head in on her.

"Yep. Let's get it!" she said and added the syringes to her bag of vampire killing accessories. It didn't get used much since she and Prince were vampire killing accessories themselves.

"I know, I know. See me in a few," Martin sighed as his parents came out. Kristine was now too strong for him to read her mind, so he had to guess.

"Yes sir, mister," she said and planted kisses all over his face. He and his father exchanged nods as they departed.

Flying is always quicker than driving, so the couple took to the air. The height advantage also allowed them to scope out the lab as well as the surrounding area. They spotted a cargo van pulling away with the essence of their child emanating from within.

"Take the truck. I'll handle the warehouse!" Kristine said before Prince could say the exact same.

"Actually I was going to let you have the truck while I took care of the warehouse," he said.

"Stop whining," she laughed and launched herself towards the truck. Kristine slammed into the moving vehicle like a missile. The force forced it into a gas station and blew up.

"Showoff!" he said as their truck did a somersault in the air. He would not be outdone, so he launched himself at their facilities below. Prince sped around the inside of the building and created a vortex. People and equipment got sucked up into the cyclone. He shot straight up the roof just as the building went up in flames. The truck explosion had nothing on the fireworks display the lab put on.

"Show off!" Kristine snarled, then laughed. The smile was wiped away when a wicked thought crossed her mind. She stripped out of her clothes and took off.

"Oh no you don't!" he said and took off after her. He stripped out of his own clothes as he took off behind her. They were high above the beautiful city of Denver when he caught up with her. They shared a giggle and a kiss before getting down to the business of pleasure.

"Back shots!" Kristine laughed as he turned her around and slid into her.

"My fave!" he said and worked his hips. He turned her back around so they could make love face to face. Make love they did for hours until the sun began to rise. The daywalkers no longer had to worry about the harmful sun rays. They just didn't want to end up on pornhub.

*****

"Next stop, Californ-i-a!" Prince said as the family loaded into the vehicle. Melcina was bundled up to protect her sensitive skin from burning in the sunlight. She hurried into the SUV so she could safely unwrap.

"Disneyland?" Martin dared.

"Of course!" his mother insisted. She wasn't worried about spoiling the boy. Let his future wife deal with it once he was older. For now, he could have whatever he wanted.

"I wanna try a couple of those rides myself. They didn't have that when I was a kid," Prince said.

"They didn't have a lot of things when you were a child!" his wife reminded and cracked up laughing. Little Martin was the only one who didn't get the joke but laughed since everyone else was laughing.

"Ha ha," he said and pulled from their hotel.

"What do you say we swing through Vegas? Check out the buffet?" Kristine suggested.

"The strip is the buffet!" Melcina cheered from the back seat. Prince nodded in agreement and drove toward Nevada. It was just after nightfall when the arrived in Sin City. The Vegas strip was illuminated like a modern day Gomorrah.

"It's so loud mommy!" Martin whined and covered his ears. He could hear the disgusting thoughts swirling in the night air. Thunderous thoughts of greed and lust that made the child blush.

"It is loud," Melcina agreed. The drumbeat of all those hearts beating was more than she could bear.

Luckily, Prince saw their dilemma and felt their pain. He hung a left on the same corner where Tupac got shot and sped away from the strip. They found a family friendly motel and booked a suite. It was now feeding time.

"I wanna try the food at one of these brothels!" Kristine announced.

"I bet," Prince said. He knew first hand just how self-righteous his wife could be. She had mentioned going to visit one of the ranches since hearing a news report about one. "I'm in the mood to gangbang."

"I wanted to check out the magic show," Melcina added while Martin hooked his portable game.

"Well, you go first. We'll stay with him until you get back," Kristine offered. Melcina was out the door in a flash.

She stepped out into the hot, desert air and inhaled. Then turned into a blur as she sped towards the casinos. The pounding heartbeats directed her inside one of the casinos directly on the strip.

"Oh my!" Melcina cheered as she looked around the smorgasbord of mortals. A large woman in the buffet line caught her attention and drew her near.

Don't make a scene she chided to herself as she closed in on her dinner, gathering her dinner.

The woman loaded a plate high with loaded baked potatoes, stuffed chicken breast, and a bloody cut of prime rib. Melcina had chosen her and had to wait to get her alone so she could feed on her. That proved it would be easier said than done. The large lady slow walked the entire plate down her mouth, then wobbled back to the long line for seconds. Then thirds and would have been fourths.

Melcina couldn't take it. She was still a young vampire and had little self-control. She was powerless over her desires and found herself drifting over to the woman on line. She could smell her fatty blood pulsing through her body as she neared.

The dining room suddenly exploded in violence as the vampire attacked. Melcina didn't even hear the screams reverberating around the room when she jumped on the large woman's back. She had to tear away layers of fatty tissue before she could reach her veins. The woman screamed and flailed in desperation but Melcina hung on.

"Grrrr!" the monster growled when she finally hit paydirt and felt a gush of hot blood enter her mouth. She sucked the sweet liquid down her throat as the woman went down. Melcina went down with her and drank while curious onlookers took footage on their phones and tablets. Some videos were uploaded before she drank her fill and stood.

Melcina let out a loud hiss at the spectators when she stood. She was in a feeding frenzy now and had no control. Blood dripped from her fangs like a lion over a fresh kill. A guard moved in to subdue her but only got subdued himself. The vampire ripped his throat away and drank. Once she was full, she bolted out a window and scurried off into the night. This was going to be a problem.

*****

"Did you find something?" Kristine asked rhetorically when Melcina arrived back to the room. She knew she wouldn't have returned had she not fed. The same burning thirst affected her so she was well aware.

"I did!" she cheered. She wanted to come clean about the mess she had made but Kristine and Prince both flew out the windows. It would have to wait until later when they returned.

"Ma, I..." Martin called when he returned from the bathroom. He scrunched his face at seeing Melcina where his parents just were. He shrugged his shoulders and went back to playing his game.

"Where you headed?" Prince asked as they hovered above the Vegas strip. The view was spectacular for those into neon lights and flashing signs. Meanwhile, the two vampires just saw cattle moving about.

"To that so-called ranch that was on the show!" she reminded. The Homewreckers Ranch was recently featured on a documentary and caught her attention. The workers bragged about breaking up families and wrecking homes.

One woman called Sugar Lips claimed she had the best pussy on the planet. One lick had men calling home like the guy on Harlem Nights. She thought it was pretty funny but Kristine didn't. Now she was flying in her direction to go pay her a visit.

Meanwhile, Prince wanted to go pay the city's gangbangers a little visit. They too had made national news with their violence. He loved the violence. Since they were about that life, they were about to die that death. An ugly, gruesome, violent death.

Kristine arrived first and landed in the parking lot. She transformed into a middle-aged white man as she walked towards the building. A smiling man exited just as she reached the door. His happy ending was written all over his face. He pulled his cell from his pocket and hit the speed dial.

"Hey, Bobby. Put your mom on the phone. Yeah, Mary. Look-it, I'm never coming home again," he said and skipped happily to his car.

"Sugar Lips please?" Kristine requested and looked up at the menu. It contained all kinds of extra that cost extra.

"I'm booked tight, but my next appointment is running late. Maybe I can squeeze you in," the woman said. Kristine missed most of what she said since her huge breast confused her. "Wait, that was funny? I'm tight, but can squeeze,you in?"

"Very," the vampire laughed through her man disguise. She followed her into a room and transformed back into herself.

"Same price for women!" Sugar demanded and produced her point of sale swipe to accept a credit card. Kristine didn't have a credit card, so she produced her fangs. "Vampires extra!"

"Vampires are extra," Kristine agreed and attacked. She sank her fangs into the huge breast. She reeled away and spit the bitter silicone from her mouth.

"Ha!" Sugar Walls yelled as she produced her crucifix. She heard it was protection from vampires but this vampire just laughed.

"You know that's a myth, right?" she asked. The question was answered by a look of confusion, so Kristine shrugged and continued with her meal. She bit the handholding the myth completely off and spit it out.

Sugar Lips socked her with all she had and ended up with one less hand. Kristine bit that one too and spit it beside the other one. She clamped on the woman's neck and bit her throat away. She could taste the cigarettes, gin, prescription pills and cum the woman ate all day as she drained her dry

"Look-it. You's ain't never coming home again either," Kristine mocked the empty shell. She transformed back into the same man as she walked out. They still had to stay under the radar from authorities who hired them to exterminate vampires. She rushed home and found Prince had beat her back.

"Hey you," Prince greeted when Kristine returned to the hotel. He looked plenty comfortable even though he had only returned a few minutes before her. Just long enough to shower the violence of the evening away and slip into his pajamas.

"Hey, yaself. Did you eat?" she greeted in return and stripped out of her clothes.

"Huh?" he asked as is she asked in a foreign language. Vampire or no vampire, she was one sexy woman.

"I asked if you ate, mister!" she laughed and blushed at his admiration. Every woman likes to know she is pleasing to her husband's eye. The look in Prince's suggested she was the apple in his.

"Did I!" he laughed and partially filled her in on the massacre he made in the hood. "Come to find out, they weren't really 'bout that life!"

CHAPTER 34

"Melcina, no!" Kristine whined when footage of her feeding on the woman in the casino was the top story.

"Excuse me," Prince said and excused himself so they wouldn't see him laughing. Sure it was a serious matter but that shit was funny as well.

"I'm sorry. I couldn't help myself!" Melcina pouted and whined. "I could hear their hearts beating so loud. Then I could taste it before I even bit her!"

"Birthday cake, huh?" Kristine heard herself say and licked her lips.

"With white icing and sprinkles! I have no idea what came over me," she pleaded as if she wanted help. Kristine knew exactly what was wrong with her. She was a vampire. A monster and there is no controlling it. Ultimately, there was either the cure or the kill. It was closing in on the time to make that choice.

Prince wasn't exactly off the hook either. He was totally off the hook himself last night and that made the news too. He didn't just feed, he ate. Literally, since unleashed the beast and transformed into his wolf. He attacked the gangs of both colors and united them in death.

"Prince!" Kristine screeched when the reports of his carnage followed that of Melcina's.

"You always in trouble," Martin said and shook his head. His patted his father on the back just in case he didn't make it back.

"Tell me about it," he said and danced out to face the music.

"Umm, what is that?" his wife demanded and pointed at the TV.

"I—" he began until the scene switched to the Homewrecker Ranch. "You tell me!"

"Really?" Kristine said of the president ordering flags to be flown at half staff in honor of the whore.

"Well, he is an idiot," Prince reminded. "Anyway, let's get out of here."

The family packed and prepared to take their show on the road. All signs led to Beverly Hills, California. The sooner they found out who was actually behind the synthetically made vampires the sooner they could get back to their lives.

Once they destroyed the rest of the vampires, they could finally live in peace. At least that was the plan. Melcina bundled up to protect herself from the sun and bolted out to the car. She and young Martin had an unspoken conversation in the back seat while Prince and Martin rode upfront. They made the drive in time to catch a splendid sunset on the Pacific Ocean.

"You see that, Martin?" Kristine asked and looked at her son in the mirror. She snapped her head around when she saw a line of blood trickle from his nostril. "What's wrong?"

"I can feel... I feel," the boy stammered, unsure of what it was that he was feeling. His father knew, though. He felt it, too.

"She's here. Katrina, she's here!" Prince said when he felt the unmistakable presence that he knew so well. It was stronger than ever. So strong the thought crossed his mind to turn the vehicle around and run for their lives.

"We can defeat her together," Kristine offered as if she had read his mind, A good wife can read her husband's face and figure out what's on his mind.

"Plus we have our secret weapon," he remembered. The diluted solution made from their son's blood was the vampire equivalent of nitrous oxide in a dragster. It would supercharge them both if need be.

"We do," she agreed and touched his hand. His chin lifted and he continued on towards their destination.

Prince was nice enough to Commandeer Butta's old house since he didn't need it any more. A Tictac container could hold what was left of him after the wolf got to him. It was fully furnished and had a couple of cars to drive. Sure beats an AirBnb.

"Watch this!" Melcina declared and hopped out of the car. Prince twisted his lips as she twirled in the fading sunlight. He wasn't impressed since the sun had already dipped below the horizon. The residue rays left were harmless.

"Nice!" Kristine cheered in encouragement. She knew the girl wanted to be a daywalker like her and Prince, but they had other plans for her. They went inside and made themselves at home and fed Martin his dinner. When the night had finished overtaking the day, it was time for the vampires to feed. Then it was time to hunt for Katrina.

"Should bring you guys something?" Melcina asked and prepared to go out into the night.

"Only thing you're bringing is me!" Kristine insisted. "After the show you put on in Vegas!"

"Like you were so subtle," Prince laughed. Not that it mattered now. If they could feel Katrina's presence, surely she could feel theirs.

"Can we hit the Hollywood strip?" Melcina asked as they stepped out to a donated Bentley. Again her social media said it was the place to be for hip young vampires. She wanted to meet some hip young vampires so she could eat them.

"We can!" Kristine replied happily for the same reason. She didn't mind the boost from killing more vampires since the showdown with Katrina was imminent. She was confident they would defeat her. She had to be since the alternative was death.

"Wish I could fly," Melcina pouted as they pulled away. She hoped tonight would be the night she became powerful enough to fly like Prince and Kristine.

"Humph," Kristine said instead of lying to her. Tonight could go either one of two ways. Neither included her being able to fly. She navigated over to the Hollywood strip and looked for some action. It didn't take long before they found some.

"Date?" Two prostitutes called out to passing cars. "Two for one special!"

"So they can tag team you dummies and drink your blood!" Melcina laughed when she heard it. The two vampires were new and weak, so they hunted in pairs. Both of their heads snapped towards the direction of the strong vampire presence. They spotted Kristine and made a run for it.

"I got them!" Melcina announced and tore out after them. After a few kills, she had more powers than these girls and caught up quickly. She followed them into a alley and pounced.

"Like a cheetah on an antelope!" Kristine cheered as she walked in behind them. Melcina had them both trapped on the pavement with her claws.

"Let us up!" one demanded. It was followed by the other who yelled, "Set us free!!

"Let's set them free," Kristine said and snatched one or the girls. She sagely snatched her throat out with her claws and began to drink. Melcina did the same and held her down and fed. She leaned back and felt her power transfer into her.

"Watch this!" Melcina declared and took to the air. She shot straight up to the top of the building. She did a twist and turn, then tumbled back towards earth.

"Not quite, chica," Kristine comforted when she landed with a thud. They had drank their fill now it was time to handle business.

*****

"His bedtime is nine o'clock no matter what he says," Kristine reiterated. Melcina looked up and squinted at her while she relayed instructions as if she were never coming back.

Martin was busy playing his game while his father packed for their mission. He loaded the "his and her" solid silver swords. The heavy metal's presence didn't affect either of them but getting cut with it was a different matter. He packed the specialized guns with bullets made from silver and laced with their son's deadly, undiluted blood.

"Don't forget these," Kristine said and packed the diluted syringes of the diluted blood. She had designed an Epi-pen type device to deliver the dose in a hurry.

"What about those?" Prince asked of similar devices containing Martin's pure blood. It would turn them both into God knows what but would ultimately kill them.

"We won't need those," she said, but packed them anyway. They peeked in on their child at play but didn't say goodbye. Just in case it was really goodbye.

"We'll have to get one of these," Prince said when they climbed into the Bentley. The car had the feel of flying first class in a aircraft.

"Yes!" Kristine cheered. The car was okay as far as she was concerned. She was just happy to hear in speaking in future tense. Tomorrow still wasn't promised so she added an "In sha Allah."

"Yeah, God willing," Prince agreed. It had been a long time since he thought about God. He could only hope God hadn't forgotten about him like he forgot about God.

Kristine cast an occasional side eye at her husband as he drove along without consulting the GPS. She knew he didn't need to since she too could feel Katrina's presence as they drove. He was headed straight towards the iconic Hollywood sign high up in the hills. The feeling got stronger the closer they got. Until a trickle of blood escaped Kristine's nostril. That's when she knew they were in trouble.

"Don't let her inside your head. Focus your thoughts on her head rolling down this hill," Prince advised and came to a stop. They grabbed their swords and got out.

"Did you bring my boy?" Katrina asked, sitting atop the "Y" in the Hollywood sign.

"Your boy? Bich, I'll—" Kristine growled and made a move to fly up to her.

"Chill," Prince advised since that would be a mistake. They needed hate to defeat her, not anger.

"You two have really hampered our plans," Katrina said as she floated down to the ground. "We have big plans for the boy."

"We?" Prince asked and looked around for the rest of "we", but saw no one.

"You're trying to turn the entire world into vampires?" Kristine announced when she got it.

"For now. Ultimately, there can be only one. Once I absorb all the powers, I will be that, one." she admitted.

"Actually, you'll be twelve or thirteen," Prince said and drew his sword so he could chop her twelve or thirteen pieces.

"Make that twenty!" Kristine said and drew hers as well.

"Have it your way," Katrina shrugged. She extended her hands and transformed them both into razor sharp swords.

Prince and Kristine weren't impressed and went on the attack. Sparks lit up the night sky as the blades clashed. The vampires moved at superhuman speed as they slashed, jabbed and thrusted. Katrina let out an eerie laugh as she twirled her swords like batons. Every time a blow was struck, the wound healed instantly. This could have gone on forever until Katrina upped the anti.

"No fair. Two against one!" she protested. Her protest was short-lived until she split herself into two. Then two more. Now it was four against two.

"Let's see how you like it," all four Katrina's said as they separated. This was time to get their guns, but they wouldn't be able.

The tide shifted and both Prince and Kristine took bloody blows. More than they could recover from. More than they would recover from. It went from bad to worse when the four Katrina's split again and became eight.

"Goodbye, Mr. and Mrs. Jones!" all eight Katrina's laugh as they closed in for the kill.

"Now!" Kristine yelled. They both pulled the syringes filled with Martin's diluted blood. They injected themselves right in the heart and supercharged themselves.

All sixteen of Katrina's eyes went wide when they morphed into huge wolves. One Katrina made a run, but Kristine swallowed her whole. Prince bit another in half before they attacked the rest.

"Oh shit!" Katrina said and took flight. She said it again when the large wolves both sprouted wings from their back and took off after her. She split into two and went in separate directions.

Prince and Kristine both took off after one. They caught their prey in mid-air and tore them to shreds. There would be no regeneration today since they swallowed the pieces. And most of blood rained down on the hillside.

Both wolves let out a mighty howl when Katrina's powers rushed into their bodies. Kristine actually had an orgasm from the rush.

"Really?" Prince laughed. Now, they where the most powerful vampires on the planet.

*****

"Awe, man!" Melcina protested when she saw what new powers Kristine developed. She was wrapped and covered to protect her from the sun while Kristine wore a sundress.

"Don't worry chica. I got you when we get home," Kristine promised. That would take a few more hours since Martin was running around the park with the other children.

He was still happy and healthy and showed no trace of being a vampire, besides reading people's thoughts. His parents were working on teaching him how to control it. He started school soon and they couldn't have him reading his teacher's mind.

The day dragged on for days as far as Melcina was concerned. They finally returned home just before dusk. Once the child ate his dinner, she was ready to go forage through the city and find hers.

"You ready?" Kristine asked when they retreated to her lab.

"I'm ready!" she cheered and bounced. She looked forward to flying around the city and feeding on mortals. Her fangs slid out in eager anticipation.

"I see!" she laughed and prepared a syringe. "Roll up your sleeve."

"Will I be a daywalker?" she asked hopefully.

"You will," Kristine said as she pushed the needle into a vein. She drew some of her vampire blood into the barrel of the syringe, then pressed the plunger sending the solution into her system. "Now, I need you to think of happy times. The best time of your life when you were little."

"And my dad used to put me on his neck when we went to the swap meet," she recalled. A huge smile spread on her face at the pleasant memory. "I could see the whole swap meet!"

"That's right," Kristine said softly. She knew how much she enjoyed being a vampire and could only hope the happy memory overrode her desire. It was the difference between the solution she injected from being a cure or a kill.

Melcina was still smiling as she drifted off into a slumber.

Well?" Prince asked when Kristine emerged from the lab alone.

"Don't know," she shrugged and cuddled up next to him. Both were hungry but neither was in the mood to feed.

Melcina was family but they could not let her remain a vampire. They were steadily eradicating vampires from the face of the planet. Eventually she would have to go, too. They drifted into their own heads until a knock on their bedroom door pulled them back into the present.

"Your turn," Kristine reminded since she had to put their son back to bed last night. He nodded to her and called out.

"Come in," Prince said and the door eased open. Instead of young Martin, a very mortal Melcina walked in.

"Awe, man!" she pouted. She was mortal once again and didn't like it one bit.

"It's the lesser of two evils," Kristine sighed. She was relieved to see the cure didn't kill her.

"Now we can eat!" Prince cheered and rolled off the bed. He and his wife set off into the night in search of prey and vampires. They would feed and kill until they were the only ones left. There would be only two.

THE END...

Epilogue

"Higher!" Melcina dared as Martin kicked and rocked on the swing. "That's high enough!" Kristine pleaded. Vampire killing vampire or not, she was still quite the worry wart when it came to her son. She carried tools of their trade in her purse but they were powerless about kids falling off of swing sets from swinging too high.

"He's fine," Prince insisted. He could protect his son from all foes but wouldn't protect him from childhood.

"Watch, this!" young Martin called from high in the air. All eyes were on him when he kicked out and did several flips on his way back down to earth. He nailed the jump and raised his hands triumphantly."Told you he's a vampire," Kristine whispered to her husband.

"That still don't mean. he's a vampire," Prince joked. His mouth opened to laugh but he stopped in his tracks. He turned to his family and yelled, "Run!"

"Take him and go!" Kristine insisted even though she didn't see and couldn't feel whatever spooked her husband. Melcina had been trained and knew exactly what to do and exactly where to go. She grabbed the boy and rushed away just as the weather changed.

A sudden cold wind pushed in dark clouds that turned day into night. The presence of the tens of thousand vampires began to descend. Kristine wisely reached into her bag for help.

"Here!" she said and produced the solution of their son's diluted blood.

"Yeah," he agreed and accepted it. This were too many vampires to fight without the boost. They both injected themselves and prepared for battle.

They watched the rolling fog for the legion of vampires on the way.

"Huh?" Kristine asked when an elderly man emerged from the fog. He was bent at the waist and had an unsteady gait.

"Look," Prince warned. The man got younger and larger with every step he took towards them.

"Where are the rest?" Kristine asked in a panic. The feeling was too intense to simply be one vampire.

"There are no more. He ate them," Prince said when he realized who the man was. "This is Count Vladimir, Katrina's husband."

"We meet at last," Vladimir said down at them since he now stood ten feet tall.

"What do you want!" Kristine demanded and tried to step in front of her husband. She would gladly die for him but had a deadly weapon so she could kill for him. The bullets were laced with Martin's vampire killing blood. Prince pulled her behind him and cocked his own weapon.

"There can be only one. With the help of your son's blood, I'll make the world my slaves," Vladimir boomed.

"Oh, you want my son's blood?" he asked and turned to his wife. "He wants our son's blood."

"Well, let's give it to him!" she laughed. Both raised their guns and emptied them into the super-sized vampire. They had used this weapon before and it killed vampires instantly. They would sizzle like bacon as it burned them from the inside out. Instead, Vladimir lolled his head back in laughter as if the thirty rounds tickled.

"My turn!" Vladimir announced and attacked. He moved on Prince first, but Kristine transformed into her wolf and lunged. The Count hit her with a casual backslap that sent her a hundred feet.

Prince made a lunge of his own, but Vladimir snatched him off of his feet. He embraced his so tightly, the sound of ribs breaking could be heard over the ominous thunder in the sky.

Kristine shook off the shock and jumped back into the fray. She drew her fangs and claws and attacked. Vladimir tossed Prince against a tree and broke his back. Luckily, the solution of Martin's blood healed his broken bones. He joined his wife and fought him

with everything they had. They were no match for him, even super-
charged by the undiluted solution.

Vladimir patted his mouth and yawned dramatically as he fend-
ed them both off with one hand. He let out an amused chuckle and
backhanded them both away. They flew another hundred feet into a
park bench.

"Now, where is the boy?" he boomed so loud, it set off a small
dust devil. The mini cyclone scooped up pigeons and squirrels as it
rolled by.

Prince and Kristine looked him, then each other. They were on
the verge of being defeated and knew he would find Martin. Kristine
reluctantly pulled the last trick from her bag of tricks. The syringes of
their son's pure blood. It would turn them into God knows what but
would very possibly kill them. Vladimir would certainly kill them, so
she handed one to her husband and injected herself with the other.

"Ah, yes. I can feel the boy!" Vladimir pronounced when they
stood. They began marching back towards him and he towards them.
Soon, they were all speeding towards destruction.

Vladimir doubled in size to twenty feet when they were within
feet of the couple. The couple transformed into a large lion and lioness. The Count tried to put on the brakes, but it was too late.

The lions stood as tall as he was with three feet long fangs and
claws. The lioness went for a leg and clamped on. She pulled it away
as the lion bit away a chunk of his midsection.

Vladimir healed himself instantly but it didn't help. The lion
pair tore him limb from limb. Prince slammed him to the ground
with a giant paw and pressed his claws into his chest while Kristine
snatched off body parts quicker than he could regenerate.

Prince felt his claw inching towards his beating heart. He let out
a mighty roar that his son heard as Melcina rushed him to their safe
house in the Bronx. Martin's head turned back to the direction of the
park.

Vladimir's eyes went wide when he felt his black heart being pulled from his chest. Both lions bit it in half and swallowed. A bolt of lighting lit the sky as Vladimir's thousand year reign had came to an end.

The clouds rolled back out and made room for the sun. Prince and Katrina shrank back into their human form while what was left of the count sizzled in the sun.

"My dear," Prince said and extended his hand. His wife took and he led her to a bench.

"He'll be fine. Melcina knows what to do," Kristine said as they sat and she laid her head on his shoulder. They had instructed Melcina on how to raise their son in case of their demise.

"Yes, fine," Prince agreed. They shared a parting kiss as their insides began to smolder. Smoke billowed from their ears and nostrils. She laid her head back on his shoulder and let out a sigh. It would be her last.

Prince took a few more breaths and joined his wife in death. Their bodies began internal combustion until they were reduced to dust. A gentle breeze whipped in and scattered their ashes over central park.

"There can be only one," young Martin said when he could longer feel his parents presence. A lone tear escaped his eye and ran down his face. It ran down his nose, over his lip and hung on his fangs.